How to Write Comedy

How to Write Comedy

BRAD ASHTON

Cartoons by
NIGEL PAIGE

ELM TREE BOOKS
London

ELM TREE BOOKS

Penguin Books Ltd, 27 Wrights Lane, London W8 5TZ (Publishing & Editorial)
and Harmondsworth, Middlesex, England (Distribution & Warehouse)
Viking Penguin Inc., 40 West 23rd Street, New York, New York 10010, U.S.A.
Penguin Books Australia Ltd, Ringwood, Victoria, Australia
Penguin Books Canada Limited, 2801 John Street, Markham, Ontario, Canada L3R 1B4
Penguin Books (N.Z.) Ltd, 182—190 Wairau Road, Auckland 10, New Zealand

First published in Great Britain 1983 by
Elm Tree Books/Hamish Hamilton Ltd

Reprinted 1987

British Library Cataloguing in Publication Data

Ashton, Brad
  How to write comedy.
  1. Comedy — Authorship
  I. Title
  808.7   PN169

ISBN 0-241-11045-9
ISBN 0-241-11092-0 Pbk

Filmset by Pioneer
Printed and bound in Great Britain by
Billing & Sons Ltd, Worcester

Contents

To my wife Valerie, who only laughs at my jokes when someone else tells them. And to all those top comedians and producers who have made the job of writing comedy so enjoyable for me.

1 / Gag Writing and Gag Switching

Despite what most people think, comedy *can* be manufactured. Indeed, there are exceedingly few comedy writers who could expect to earn a living relying on inspiration alone. Just about every gag or joke you hear has been 'built' by someone. And that person had the very same raw materials as you have at your disposal right now. This chapter will show you how to use those raw materials to create comedy.

Experienced writers soon develop their own methods of thinking up gags, but the one about to be outlined is the most frequently used and the easiest to master. To illustrate it best, let's select a subject that most of us are familiar with because it's become part of our daily lives — the automobile.

Having chosen our subject we make a list of everything we

can think of that is in any way associated with it. Such a list would include:—

Engine	Small Car	Fan Belt
Wheels	Oil	Battery
Dashboard	Hubcaps	Foreign
Traffic	Mileage	Headlamps
Accident	Bonnet	Pedestrians
Parking	Gears	Anti-Freeze
Speed	Speedometer	Number Plates
Towing	Air Filter	Steering Wheel
Chassis	Radiator	Cigarette Lighter
Tyres	Traffic Cop	Women Drivers
Upholstery	Petrol	Second Hand
Paintwork	Boot	Road Holding
Large Car	Seats	Spark Plugs

You can probably think of others, but this is enough to work from.

Undoubtedly the easiest form of gag to invent is the one that uses the *exaggeration* technique. If we want to exaggerate the size of a car, the best way to do it is to add another element for comparison. We've all seen advertisements for 'Five Minute Car Washes', so if we merge that thought with the size of the car we'd have, 'This car is so long it takes twenty minutes to get through a five minute car wash.' Some cars fold down into a bed in the back . . . 'This car is so long it doesn't have a bed in the back, it has a whole dormitory.'

Alternatively we can go the other way and exaggerate how small the car is. The thought here is that the car is so small it can be carried around on one's person. So we look for something else that is carried around on one's person and produce the gag, 'This car is made for women drivers. Instead of having to park it they just hitch it on to their charm bracelet.' Or another version, 'The car's so small it costs just £1,500. And that even includes the carrying case.'

Go back to your list and see what other words lend themselves to easy exaggeration. The glove compartment is one. 'The car's so small the glove compartment only holds three fingers.' Another one could be, 'The car's so small the cigarette lighter only lights butts.'

Getting the point across that the car is small could be done by associating it with a baby. 'The car's so small that if you flood the engine all you have to do is put it over your shoulder and burp it.'

Probably the next easiest form of gag is the *word play*. Not to be confused with the *pun* which we will deal with next. In word plays you lead your audience to think you mean a word to be taken one way and then reveal it's to be taken in a different way. Using the word 'engine' again we could say 'I'm late here today because my car had engine trouble. It stalled on a railway crossing and got hit by an engine.' Another version, 'Our star hasn't arrived here yet because he's had fan belt trouble. One of his fans belted him.' The earliest example I remember of this was hearing a comedian say, 'I hear Liberace's been hitting the bottle a lot lately. He can't get his perfume open.' Since 'hitting the bottle' is another way of saying that someone drinks a lot . . . and perfume is sold in bottles . . . the gag worked well. It was a successful word play.

Some sage once said that people groan at puns because they didn't think of them first. Certainly there are painful puns like the one about the fisherman's wife who said, 'Not tonight, dear, I've got a haddock.' But clever puns are much respected and comedians like Groucho Marx would have been lost without them. Remember him saying to a bank manager, 'You wouldn't float me a loan, but you could at least float me a kidney.' Or to the restaurant manager, 'The food here gave me ptomaine poisoning. It started at my main toe and worked its way up.' Or about the society debutante, 'Say, that girl's well reared. And the front of her isn't too bad either.'

When comedian Ronnie Corbett was honoured at Buckingham Palace he told the waiting press reporters, 'It was all over in a minute. Then the Queen swept down the staircase . . . dusted the curtains and polished the furniture.'

If we want to stick with the subject of cars we could refer to the two main motoring organisations and say, 'Because of the large number of breakdowns this year both the A.A. and the R.A.C. are up on their tows.' Or, 'The car driver was so angry he lifted the bonnet of the vehicle and threw something at the pedestrian. The charge was assault with battery.' The word battery can itself be the source of a pun in 'I paid cash for everything except the battery. I charged that.'

Our fourth form of gag is the *twisted cliche*. That's where we use a well known phrase or saying and give it a new twist. 'If all the cars on the road were laid end to end . . . it would be a Sunday afternoon.' 'Give a woman an inch . . . and she'll make a bathing costume out of it.' 'Mary had a little lamb . . . beef was too expensive.'

Confining ourselves to cars again we'd remember that meter feeding is a hazard to the motorist. Hence 'If you think the automobile is here to stay, . . . try feeding the parking meter.' Used cars have a bad reputation for reliability, so how about this thought: 'It's hard to drive a bargain . . . especially when it's a used car.' In each case what we've done is think of some aspect of the car and then find a cliche to marry it up with. But the process can be reversed, like this: 'In the spring a young man's fancy turns . . . could get him a ticket for dangerous driving.'

A fifth form of gag is the *reverse gag*. It works by just reversing the normal routine of the subject. Every time my car's serviced I always insist on an oil change. I could say that 'My car's in such a bad state now that the mechanic advised me to keep the oil and change the car.' Or 'The car's in such a bad state that now when I turn the engine on the fan belt stays still and the car spins round.' And we all know the gag of the Arab who's so rich that when he makes out a cheque the bank bounces.

Then there's what's known as *illogical logic*. 'The man arrested for putting a foreign coin in a parking meter pleaded not guilty because it was for a foreign car.' And the Irishman who complained 'That garage charged me £14 for towing me just one mile. But I got my own back. I kept my brakes on all the way.' Both of these sound logical to the person in the gag, but to the listener, they are illogical. And that's what makes them funny.

The *insult* form is mostly applied to people, but can be applied to cars just as well. 'That car's in such a bad condition, if it were a horse it would have to be shot.' 'That car's like a baby. It won't go anywhere without its rattle.' Notice how often I use something else like the horse or baby to make comparison with the car in order to create the gag.

Sometimes forms of gags overlap. Here's an example of a word play that also doubles as an insult. 'That car's so old it doesn't have an exhaust pipe. After 200 yards the whole car gets exhausted.'

With cars as our subject we have a vast area for insult gags. We can extend the subject to include drivers, mechanics, manufacturers etc. 'The current popular phrase is "Right on", but in the case of De Lorean it's "Write-Off".' 'That car looks like something that Rolls built while Royce wasn't looking.' Here's a combination of pun and insult. 'That car is built so low it's enough to give Mercedes the Benz.'

Women drivers in particular are an easy target for gag writers, perhaps unfairly. One female wit said, 'A woman driver is a person who drives like a man, only she gets blamed for it.' And she added, 'If women are such bad drivers, it's probably because their husbands taught them.'

That lady may well be right, but here are some gags to illustrate what a comedy writer would make of the subject. 'My wife has such a poor sense of direction that she goes the wrong way even on a two-way street.' 'The way my wife drives she doesn't need a seat belt. What she needs is a straitjacket.' 'They're coming out with a special model for women drivers. It has a pre-dented bumper.' 'What my wife doesn't know about driving would fill a hospital.' 'My wife does quite well with her car. She's getting forty miles to the bumper.' 'What I want out of my new car is — my wife in the driving seat.' 'When two cars are double parked it's easy to tell which was parked by a woman. It's the one on top.'

Insult gags about women and cars do not have to focus on driving skills. The thought that some girls won't go out with a boy who hasn't got a car can be expressed like this: 'The only time women walk these days is when they march down the aisle.' Or you could cash in on the popular belief that most wives are back seat drivers with, 'If you really want to stop that noise in your ear — let her drive.' And, 'I've had special seat belts installed in my car. The one on my wife's side straps over her mouth.'

Women's shyness about their age provides another tie-in with cars. 'Most women drive slower than men. They always want to stay under thirty.' Or 'Women are like cars. If they've had a good paint job, it's difficult to tell their real age.' And there's the 'dumb blonde' approach. 'My wife bought a new car and filled out the insurance form. She reached the part which said, "The company must be notified of an accident as soon as possible." She wanted to know how soon after buying the car she had to have an accident.' Women have the reputation about being fussy over decorations. That sparks off the thought, 'My wife's too interested in interior decorating. Now she even wants to re-arrange the seats in my car.'

Time to move on to the next gag form which is the *sex gag*. This does not have to be too smutty or risqué. It just has to connect the thought of sex and automobiles. It could be as innocuous as this twisted cliche: 'A miss in the car is worth two in the engine.' Or: 'Do you remember back to the old days when the only problem you had with parking was getting the girl to agree?' Or: 'Whenever I take my girl for a ride and park the car, right away she tries to start something. The engine.'

Before finally leaving automobiles let me apply just one more form of gag, the *topical*. Every October we have the Motor

Show and every year the number of road accidents increases. So putting these two thoughts together we have, 'Every October I visit the Motor Show. I like to see what's going to knock me down next year.' 'I can tell the Japs have made a big inroad into the British car market. Every other vehicle I see has slanted headlamps.'

*　　*　　*

Let's leave cars now and move on to another subject we all know about — doctors.

In thinking of words associated with doctors, we may well come up with 'X-Ray'. There's an immediate funny thought if one pictures a doctor standing behind an X-Ray machine lecturing to a group of students and asking, 'Do I make myself clear?'

Doctors prescribe medicine and the labels often say, 'Keep this bottle tightly closed.' Take it at its literal meaning and you could have a patient tell his doctor, 'I didn't take any of the medicine, doctor. The label said "Keep the bottle tightly closed", so I did.'

The phrase 'Is there a doctor in the house?' is universally known. We can switch it and have a doctor come out of his surgery into his crowded waiting room and ask, 'Is there an undertaker in the house?'

We know that many doctors hate making housecalls. Indeed one father said he knew his son was going to be a doctor because he never came when called. You could have a doctor tell his patient on the phone, 'Sorry, I don't make house calls, but why don't you drop in and see me when you're feeling better.'

Again on the subject of house calls. A patient could phone his doctor and say, 'My wife seems to have dislocated her jaw. If you could stop by in a week or two, there's no hurry. . . . .'

Or supposing a doctor is found in bed with a woman patient, he might say to her irate husband, 'I'd appreciate it if you didn't mention this to anybody. I can't have everyone expecting me to make house calls.'

Most doctors are now insisting on the appointment system. And many of them are so busy patients are having to book an appointment to book an appointment. You can imagine a doctor being told by his angry patient, 'I'm sorry I didn't phone for an appointment last week, but I didn't know I was going to break my leg till this morning.'

In Britain medical services are free. Americans claim they

spend billions of dollars a year on health alone. And what they have to show for it is just a lot of healthy doctors.

Health and wealth. An illustration of American medical costs could be along these lines. A doctor tells his patient needing surgery, 'Don't worry about the cost of the operation. Just pay me five hundred dollars down and three hundred a month for the next three years.' The patient says, 'Sounds just like buying a car.' And the doctor replies, 'You're right, I am!'

You'd probably get a laugh if you had two American doctors leaning sadly over a patient and one commenting, 'I'm afraid it's a hopeless case. The poor fellow has no medical insurance.' Or reverse the situation and have the worried patient looking up at the serious expressioned doctor and asking, 'Is it something I can afford?'

Diets are associated with doctors too, so let's mix the thought of money and diet together and we'll come up with something like, 'I'm putting you on a strict diet, Mr Ashton. That's so you can save up to pay my bill.'

There are many types of doctors. A list of them would certainly include dermatologists (skin doctors). Have you ever thought — do dermatologists ever make rash decisions? Or do tree surgeons ever go out on a limb?

Psychiatrists have been described as doctors who only listen to you if you don't make sense. Link this with people who talk to their plants. A man tells his psychiatrist, 'My wife is really weird, she talks to our plants.' The doctor says, 'So what? Lots of people talk to their plants.' And the husband comes back with, 'By telephone?'

Marriage and psychiatry go well together in gag form. Here are some quick examples. A man tells his doctor, 'My wife says I have a persecution complex. But of course, she hates me.' Or a woman says, 'I can't communicate with my husband. I can't communicate with my son. I can't communicate with my daughter . . . Doctor, are you listening to me?'

Here's a gag that lends itself to an easy switch. 'Doctor, my wife says I have a superiority complex. Tell me, what's your humble opinion?' Switch the complexes and you have, 'This inferiority complex I have, doctor, it's not a very good one, is it?'

Extend the earlier persecution complex gag a stage further. The psychiatrist could say, 'Mr Ashton, how long have you felt — take those dirty shoes off my couch — persecuted?' Or even, 'Believe me, height is only a mental hang-up. Just think of yourself as being tall, Shorty.'

Doctors are a perfect subject for what's known as the

vernacular gag. This form of gag is self explanatory in the following examples:

The doctor examined the prostitute and said, 'You need a complete rest. Stay out of bed for a few days.'

The doctor examined the plumber and said, 'Let me put it to you this way — all that cholesterol is clogging up your pipes.'

The doctor examined the seriously ill bull fighter and said, 'I hope you're ready for the moment of truth.'

The doctor examined the TV repair man and said, 'I don't like your colour. I'm going to have to take you in for a while.'

The doctor examined the monk and said, 'Never mind your vow of silence. Say "Ah"'.

The doctor examined the store Santa Claus and said, 'Stick your tongue out and say "Ho-ho-ho"'.

The doctor examined the chef and said, 'To put it in layman's language, you've got braised kidneys.'

The doctor told the stockbroker he'd both good and bad news for him. 'Your pulse is down two, but your heartbeat's up three.'

The doctor told the cricketer, 'Take it easy or this could be your last innings.'

The doctor told the fat golfer, 'I'm afraid you're eight inches over par.'

The doctor told the flirtatious husband, 'Avoid all excitement. For the next six months only make love to your wife.'

The doctor told the car mechanic, 'Of course, that's only a rough estimate. We don't know what else we'll find when we open you up.'

The doctor, injecting the pilot in the rear said, 'O.K. it's over and ouch!'

The doctor examined the army general and said, 'Just try to look on these haemorrhoids as an attack from the rear.'

And finally . . . The doctor told the entomologist (student of insects), 'No, Mr Ashton, when I said bring me a specimen I didn't mean a butterfly with a pin through it.'

*   *   *

Here's another subject for creating gags about — smoking. By now you ought to be able to just analyse the gags and follow the thought process behind them.

Did you hear about the habitual cigar smoker who had to give up playing the clarinet? Before every number, he bit off the end.

You can always tell when people are substituting boiled sweets for smoking. They grind the wrapper out with their foot.

I can't get over the way the price of cigarettes keeps going up. Yesterday I bought a packet of twenty and told the tobacconist, 'I'm sorry, but all I have on me is a £5 note.' He said, 'That's all right, you can pay me the rest tomorrow.'

Cigarettes are getting so expensive now. I know one fellow who only smokes three a day — but he stains his fingers just to impress his neighbours.

There's no truth to the rumour that the Yellow Pages are just telephone directories that smoke too much.

I'll say one thing for smoking 50 cigarettes a day. It gives your hands something to do — shake!

Personally, I quit smoking — and I mean really quit. No ifs, no ands, no butts.

I once had an uncle who was the sloppiest tobacco chewer who ever lived. Died of cancer of the waistcoat.

I haven't had a cigarette since January, and the only after-effect has been a certain dryness of the throat. Comes from your tongue hanging out.

Believe me, it isn't as hard as you think to give up smoking. All you need is will power, determination and wet matches.

9

Naturally you substitute other things for smoking. I won't say what, but I am now buying whisky in packets of twenty.

You know, people who give up smoking have the same problem as people spending their first day in a nudist camp. What do you do with your hands?

I won't say what fifteen years of smoking has done to my lungs, but curtain companies are using them for patterns.

The tobacco industry is working on its first all-vegetable cigarette which consists of nothing but lettuce. It won't have a filter — just mayonnaise.

I think that smoking's unnatural. After all, if God had meant us to smoke he would have given us chimneys.

The cigarette health hazard is even more worrying to the Ku Klux Klan. They've started burning filter crosses.

I think you have enough samples of gags on smoking for you to be able to come up with a few more of your own.

*   *   *

There are new subjects for gags coming along all the time, and even some old subjects disappearing because they're no longer funny. When TV first became popular in the early 1950s there were dozens of gags being cracked about people developing square eyeballs. There were gags about the inception of jet planes. About cars and buses replacing horses. About electric trains replacing steam engines. They're all history now.

Their place was taken by gags about astronauts, rocket launchers, heart transplants, digital watches, Women's Liberation, the Concorde, oil prices, phone tapping, etc.

There are some perennial subjects that comedians feel safe with because they know their audiences are currently familiar with them. Such subjects as the high cost of living. Food prices are rocketing every week. 'At one time the most expensive walk a man could take was down the aisle of a church. Now it's the aisle of a supermarket.' Added to that could be, 'Prices have risen so fast lately my local supermarket phoned me this morning and offered to buy back all the groceries I bought last week — at twice the price.' 'Food's so high we're being asked to pay an arm and a leg for a wing and a breast.' 'If you see someone laughing at the price of meat today, it has to be a vegetarian.'

Automation is a popular subject that is familiar to all. Its many facets mean it will provide much fodder for humour. Asking ourselves what we know about automation should procure answers such as these. It causes unemployment by being used to replace people. It is supposed to be labour saving. It speeds up production. It does not take time off for coffee breaks, holidays or illness. It allows us more leisure time. It gives us computers that spew out cards with coded holes in them. It's become so sophisticated now that the machines are almost human.

That's probably enough to work with. Let us exaggerate some of those points and possibly join one or two together and see what we come up with.

1. (The machines are labour saving — but they're expensive): 'There are so many labour-saving appliances on the market today. Trouble is you have to work yourself to death to pay for them.'

2. (The automation industry is still growing): 'Everything is automated these days. Yesterday I got an obscene phone call from a recording.'

3. (They could never be completely human): 'Automation will never replace my brother-in-law. They haven't come up with a machine yet that does absolutely nothing.'

4. (Machinery often goes wrong): 'The new inventions have provided us with leisure time for reading. Especially the Yellow Pages under Repairs.'

5. (It causes unemployment): 'Automation has opened up for thousands of skilled employees a whole new world of . . . unemployment.' Or: 'Automation speeds things up. Especially the unemployment rate.'

6. (It replaces humans): 'When the spinster secretary saw the new computer she said, "I know it's supposed to replace 12 men — but I'd rather have the men!"'

* * *

Another subject worthy of consideration is flying. What does flying bring to mind? Lost luggage. Late take-offs and long delays at airports. Concorde doing 1,300 miles an hour. Plastic food. In-flight films. No smoking areas. Jet lag. Bad weather. Parachutes. Cheap flights on impoverished airlines. Let's play around with some of those thoughts.

1. (Lost luggage): 'When I fly I like to take a window seat because there are so many things to see . . . like your luggage being loaded on to another plane.' Or: 'Do you realise that in 1942 the first commercial flight around the world took a full 35 days. Now it can be done in one day. But it still takes 35 days to find where they've sent your luggage.' Or: 'Nowadays I don't book Club or Tourist or Cabin Class, I always fly freight. That's because I found that my luggage winds up in better places than I do.' (And Bob Hope said, 'I've got one piece of baggage that's done 9,000 miles more than I have.')

2. (In-Flight films): 'The flight was so bumpy that 83 people were airsick. 75 were passengers and the other eight were in the film.' Or: 'I flew to New York by Concorde and it still took four and a half hours. The pilot kept flying round and round Kennedy Airport waiting for the film to finish.'

3. (Concorde's speed combined with late take-offs): 'The one thing I can never understand about these supersonic jets is how anything that goes at 1,300 miles an hour can be two hours late in arriving.'

4. (Jet lag): 'The one thing about flying that drives me mad is the jet lag. It completely throws my timing. I sit down to dinner and I'm sexy . . . then I go to bed and I'm hungry.'

5. (Travel sickness again): 'I hate long journeys by plane. They terrify me. I get airsick when I lick an Air Mail stamp.'

6. (Confidence in the pilot): 'I lost all confidence in the pilot when he left his cabin to go to the toilet and got lost on the way.'

7. (Expensive travel): 'Travelling by plane brought something into my life I never had before. Poverty!'

8. (Cheap travel): 'I went on one of those no-frills air trips where they find ways to cut the costs. I didn't realise how much they economise till we finished the meal and had to queue up to wash our own paper plates.' Or: 'The only way to get really cheap travel is to take one of those "Go now—pay later" trips and don't come back.' 'The airline saves money by not paying any landing fees. When you get to your destination they push you out the door with a parachute.' 'Instead of films they show slides.'

9. (Mechanical failure): 'I flew to New York in one of those Jumbo jets with over four hundred passengers on board . . . with all their luggage. We had to make a forced landing in Shannon. I found out why later. The plane got a hernia.'

*   *   *

We'll take one more subject to work through this way. Christmas. The things that immediately come to mind are: Santa Claus. Presents. Shopping. The Christmas spirit. The Christmas Club. Mistletoe. Christmas cards. Snow. You can probably think of a lot more.

1. (Presents): 'I'm going to give money instead of gifts this year. It's a hell of a lot cheaper.' Or: 'It's always better giving presents than receiving them. That way you don't have to queue up for hours at the shop to exchange them after Christmas.' 'I once got an inspiration and sent someone a partridge in a pear tree, and do you know what I got in return? A summons from the RSPCA.' 'I spent weeks trying to think what to give a girl who has everything. Then I got a great idea — me!'

2. (Drinking): 'Christmas is the time to take a celebratory drink. I've had three Christmases I'll never forget — and about five I'll never remember.'

3. (Santa Claus): 'Many adults still believe in Santa Claus. They're called Maggie Thatcher supporters.' Or: 'When I was a kid I lost all respect for Santa Claus. Everywhere I went I kept seeing the old fellow at a different department store. How can you respect anyone like that who can't keep a steady job?'

4. (Christmas cards): 'Aren't Christmas cards expensive now! I used to send a card with every gift. Now the card *is* the gift!'

13

5. (Christmas Club — and presents): 'I joined a Christmas Club. It's marvellous. Every week you put a little away, and before you know it, you've saved enough money to pay for last year's presents.'

6. (Christmas shopping): 'My wife's a great Christmas shopper. She goes to the shops and comes back with everything but money. The way she shopped last year at Selfridges they thought she was taking inventory.' 'Thanks to my wife they cancelled their January Clearance Sale. They didn't have anything left.'

7. (Posting presents — and toys): 'I found a great scheme this year to find out if the toys I buy for my kids are really unbreakable. I send them by post.' Or: 'Last year I bought my son an indestructible toy that really was. He left it in the driveway and it broke my car.'

8. (The cost of toys): 'My daughter told me for Christmas she wanted a talking doll. Before I could buy it I had to go to my listening bank.'

9. (Political tie-up): 'Christmas is a time of good news and bad news. The good news is that parliament goes into recess over the holidays. The bad news is that they come back.'

10. (Santa Claus again): 'I know that at Christmas my house will be visited by the tall, jolly, bearded character with a big bag over his shoulder. My wife's brother home from university with his dirty laundry.'

*　　　*　　　*

Traffic problems . . . overcrowded housing conditions . . . crooked politicians . . . poor education facilities . . . air pollution . . . rising crime figures . . . women's fashions . . . all these are perennial subjects for comedy.

It's always a bonus when you can join two of them together. For instance, if heart transplants and soaring mortgage rates are current news you could combine them with, 'The Chairman of a mortgage company offered his heart to a hospital for transplant. He was refused. They didn't believe he had one.'

*　　　*　　　*

We've all heard it said that there are only seven basic jokes, but nobody to my knowledge has ever been able to name the seven. There are certainly more than seven basic forms for gags and jokes. In fact there are hundreds. Here are just fifteen forms with examples. Some have already been covered when we dealt with automobiles, but it should be helpful to see them being applied to other subjects as well.

1.   **Exaggeration** My uncle's nose is so big he only has to breathe in once and it lasts him all day.

2.   **Underplaying** I never could understand why they made all that fuss about the Queen's coronation. I mean, you can see a woman trying on a new hat anytime.

3.   **Illogical Logic** I never could understand why they make you put an extra stamp on an envelope that's overweight. It only makes it heavier.

4.   **The Pun** Every day I do a half hour work out on my vaulting horse. This morning I fell off. But I'm not blaming the horse. It was my own vault.

5.   **The Insult** My wife's so ugly I only look her in the face when I want to cure my hiccoughs.

6.   **Word Play** Everyone's going on strike these days. Can you imagine what would happen if all the farmers suddenly decided to stop growing? Yes, we'd have a glut of midget farmers.

7.   **The Picture** (The gag builds up a mental picture) Did you hear about the karate enthusiast who joined the army? He killed himself learning to salute.

8.   **The Self Insult** At school I was in a class of my own. All the other kids got promoted.

9.   **Word Association** My local cinema manager's started playing poker each evening so he can occasionally say he's had a full house.

10.   **The Reverse** There's a sign outside the income tax office, it says, 'Sorry — we're open.'

11.   **The Twisted Cliche** Half a loaf is better than . . . working for a living.

12.   **Truthfulness** There are two kinds of people who try to dodge paying their taxes. Men and women.

13.   **Topical** I know our country's economy's in trouble. I just got a cheque from the government and it said 'Do not fold, bend, staple, mutilate — or cash.'

14.   **The Sex Gag** My wife's so frigid we bought a water bed and she froze it.

15.   **Personalised** They put up a monument to Norman Wisdom, but it keeps falling down.

   Other forms of gags include dialect, racial, religious, sick, satirical and lots more.

*   *   *

So far we've dealt with inventing gags, now let's talk about switching gags that already exist. They can be gags that you've heard somewhere or found in a joke book. What you have to do is take the idea of the gag and then transfer it to another subject or venue so that it won't be recognisable as the same gag. Here are some examples of gags that are derived from the very same thought:

1.   Did you hear about the executive who set an example for his employees during an economy drive? He cut his afternoon nap down to thirty winks.

Switch: After a stirring speech on economy, the speaker was given two rousing cheers.

2.   I stayed at a boarding house that had two keyholes in every door. One for the key and the other for the landlady.

Switch: The landlady at my boarding house always keeps a kettle boiling on the stove. Half is for tea and the other half for steaming our mail open.

3. Thank heavens this is still a free country where a man is free to do exactly as his wife pleases.

Switch: As the woman said to her henpecked husband, 'When I want your opinion, I'll give it to you.'

4. Last night on TV they showed a Western that was so old it starred a Greek cowboy on a wooden horse.

Switch: Last night on TV they showed a Liz Taylor film that was so old she still had an English accent.

5. That hotel is so posh they won't even let you into the swimming pool without a collar and tie.

Switch: That barber shop is so exclusive they won't let you in unless you've already had a shave.

In all those cases the 'switch gag' was inspired by the idea of the first one. A lot of people think that the term gag only applies to jokes used by solo comedians. That's not so. It applies to double acts too. Here are some examples of double act gags, followed by switches on them.

1. *Comedian:* I had a great cabin on the cruise ship. It even had a built-in washing machine in the wall.
    Feed: Washing machine? That was the port hole.
    Comedian: Oh, no wonder I never got my clothes back.

2. *Comedian:* I'm not the least bit superstitious.
    Feed: Oh no? What would you do if you were walking down the street on Friday 13th and you walked under a ladder at the same time as a black cat ran out in front of you?
    Comedian: It wouldn't bother me at all. I'd just throw a little salt over my shoulder and keep on walking.

3. *Feed:* I'm still on the sunny side of forty.
    Comedian: You'd better watch out. You're getting awfully sunburnt.

4. *Feed:* Why do you bother to see those sexy films at your age?
    Comedian: Look. Dan Maskell doesn't play tennis anymore, but he's still interested in the game.

5. *Feed:* Don't worry about etiquette at the dinner table. Just watch your hostess and use the same fork as she does.
   Comedian: Isn't that rather unsanitary?

6. *Comedian:* I was playing golf this morning and I sank the putt with my first stroke.
   Feed: That's great.
   Comedian: Not really. I missed the hole and sank it in the river.

7. *Feed:* That pretty blonde won't waste her time falling for just any man. When it comes to love she wants a real man to kindle her flame.
   Comedian: Shake hands with the old lamplighter.

8. *Feed:* I read in the paper today that some archaeologists are still searching for the missing arm of the Venus de Milo.
   Comedian: Good idea. Maybe if they fix that statue up it'll be worth something.

9. *Comedian:* My wife's gone all strange. She thinks she's a taxi cab.
   Feed: Are you going to have her cured?
   Comedian: What for? It saves taking the bus.

10. *Comedian:* I thought up an idea today that'll stop me being bothered by the traffic problems in London.
    Feed: What's the idea?
    Comedian: I'm moving to Wigan.

11. *Feed:* What were you doing at the shoe shop this morning?
    Comedian: I was trying to buy a pair of alligator shoes.
    Feed: Did you get a pair?
    Comedian: No. They didn't have my alligator's size.

12. *Comedian:* Do you know what we're having for supper tonight? A lovely purloin steak.
    Feed: You mean sirloin. Purloin means stolen.
    Comedian: How else do you think we could eat steak on what we earn?

Those were the gags, now for the switching.
Number 1 was funny because the comedian hadn't realised

18

that what he thought was a washing machine was really a port hole. Let's change the subject to music.

1. *Comedian:* I've been connected with music all my life. In fact, I used to hold the piano stool for Yehudi Menuhin.
   Feed: But Menuhin is a violinist.
   Comedian: Oh, so that's why he never sat down.

We could make the subject films:

   Comedian: I'm in the film business. I'm a lighting man at MGM Studios at Elstree.
   Feed: But those studios closed down over ten years ago.
   Comedian: They did? I thought it was a long coffee break.

Now let's make it bathing:

   Feed: You're looking very clean today.
   Comedian: I just took a bath in that enormous bathtub at the YMCA
   Feed: That's not a bathtub. That's a swimming pool.
   Comedian: Oh, I wondered why I was the only one with no clothes on.

They're all the same basic gag dressed differently. Gag number 2 was funny because the comedian insisted he wasn't all that superstitious, but he proved he was by saying he'd throw salt over his shoulder. Let's change it to horoscopes:

2. *Comedian:* Those people who say they can predict the future are all fakes. One of them just cheated me out of £10.
   Feed: If I were you I'd call the police.
   Comedian: I can't. My horoscope said, 'Do nothing rash today.'

Number 3 was the old formula of using the feed line to insult the straight man about his age. We can change it to another subject that people are just as sensitive about.

3. *Feed:* I've got good hair. That's because I take care of it.
   Comedian: Sure. You lock it up in the drawer every night.

Gag number 4 was the comedian explaining away his harmless lecherous thoughts by more or less saying that while dogs chase cars, they can't drive. Here we actually keep the subject, but get a new gag out of it by changing the analogies.

4. *Feed:* You shouldn't keep looking at other women. You're a married man.
    Comedian: Yes, but just because I'm on a diet doesn't mean I can't study the menu.

Or putting it another way:

> *Feed:* You've only just got married and already you're looking at other women.
> *Comedian:* Well I only gave my bride my heart — not my eyeballs.

Number 5 is funny because the comedian takes his partner's instructions much too literally. We can change the subject to clothes, with this gag:

5. *Feed:* The Golf Club is very fussy about formal attire. If you're coming as a guest you'd better wear the same blazer as I am.
    Comedian: Is it big enough for both of us to get into?

Or, stretching the idea a little further:

> *Feed:* Don't worry about formalities at my place. We never bother to dress for dinner.
> *Comedian:* Well, that's one way to keep the soup stains off your clothes.

Gag number 6 relied on misleading the audience into thinking that the comedian had holed in one and then having him admit that he'd hit the ball into the river. Let's see how easily this switches to cars.

6. *Comedian:* Sorry I'm late. I missed the bus.
    Feed: I thought you were coming by car?
    Comedian: I did. I missed the bus and hit a lamp post.

Gag 7 has the comedian boasting about his prowess with women by exaggerating the example given in the feed line. Here's the same gag with a change of subject:

7.   *Feed:* They say you get rich by knowing how to shave
     expenses.
     Comedian: That's right. Shake hands with the head barber.

A further example is:

   Feed: They say that a really experienced man can read a
   woman like a book.
   Comedian: I know. Shake hands with the head librarian.

Number 8 had its humour in the comedian not knowing that
the Venus de Milo is already of great value. All we need to do
here is change the work of art.

8.   *Feed:* Do you know what I liked best about Paris? The
     Eiffel Tower.
     Comedian: Yes, but isn't it a shame? The framework of the
     building has been up for over 70 years and they still
     haven't put the plaster on it.

In Number 9 the fun lies in the suggestion that the wife not
only thinks she is a taxi cab, but actually gives cab rides too. If
we make the wife believe she's something else we can come up
with a gag like this:

9.   *Comedian:* My wife has this crazy notion she's a refrigera-
     tor.
     Feed: Don't worry, she'll soon get over it.
     Comedian: I hope so. She sleeps with her mouth open and
     that little white light keeps me awake all night.

Gag number 10 sets up a problem and claims to have solved
it by ignoring it. So a switch on this one could be:

10.   *Feed:* Why did you get in so late last night?
      Comedian: Well, it was the anniversary celebration at my
      club and our President insisted that we had to finish
      drinking no later than 10.30.
      Feed: So what happened?
      Comedian: At 9.30 we elected a new President.

Number 11 was a literal translation gag. The same formula
would work thus:

11.   *Comedian:* When I was in London recently I visited

Buckingham Palace. They've got four armed guards
there. Very strange.

Feed: What's so strange about that?

Comedian: I've never seen guards with four arms before.

The final one, gag number 12, relies on what at first seems
like the use of a wrong word, querying it, and then justifying it
as having been right in the first place. We'll switch the subject
from expensive meats to tramps:

12.   *Comedian:* My uncle's a tramp. He sleeps out in the fields,
      but yesterday the police came and arrested him for
      fragrancy.

      Feed: You mean vagrancy. Fragrancy's a smell.

      Comedian: I know. They were cow fields he'd been sleeping
      in.

As an exercise, I suggest you try taking the subject of
children and see how many gags you can get out of it. Also see
if you can twist or switch any of the gags in this chapter to fit in
with children.

To start you off here's a brief list of words that could be
associated with the subject:

School	Toys	Games
Swings	Slides	Roundabouts
Paper Rounds	Pocket Money	Punishment
Clothes Sizes	Homework	Accidents
School Grades	Dirty Necks	Naughtiness
Child Psychology	Teeny Boppers	Children's Television
Parents	Fighting	Cribbing
Cunning	Measles	Holidays
Playroom	Fibbing	Reports
Skipping	Prefect	Teenagers
Height	Truancy	Sweets
Crying	Dunce	Innocence
Fireworks	Bedtime	Sneak

Add as many other words as you can think of yourself, and
start writing your own gags.

2 / Routining and Tailoring Gags

This chapter deals with routining gags, so let's start right off with a selection of gags on a subject and then try to put them into a routine that a stand-up comedian could perform. The subject is oil prices.

1. Oil's so expensive now that bank robbers are forming getaway carpools.

2. You used to insure the car to cover the passengers. Now it's to cover the petrol.

3. It's so expensive, yesterday I saw a police car chasing a stolen van and both drivers were out behind pushing.

4. It's so bad, one fellow this week was mugged for the fuel in his lighter.

5.   If petrol prices go any higher I won't be able to afford my car payments.

6.   The Germans and Japanese tried to overthrow us a few years ago by taking our possessions. The Arabs are smarter — they're buying them.

7.   I used to go to a garage and say, 'Fill her up.' Now I just say, 'Give me £20's worth.'

8.   The price is so high I went to one garage and asked for a pound's worth of petrol and they just sprayed some behind my ear.

9.   Petrol prices are so high that the new owners' handbooks include a section on hitch-hiking.

10.   The British Prime Minister has been invited to Saudi Arabia because the Arabs want to meet the person who runs their country.

11.   One garage had a sign: 'Only £1 a gallon.' But that was just for water.

12.   I don't want to start rumours, but I hear that some oil companies drill dry holes on purpose. Makes a great place to hide their money.

13.   My car must be growing. When I first got it it only held £4's worth of petrol. Now it holds £16.

14.   In Las Vegas they have a filling station that only charges a dollar a gallon. But to actually get the petrol you have to put a silver dollar in the pump, pull down the nozzle, and be lucky enough to get three lemons come up.

15.   I just found out why a lot of garages close now on Sundays. It's so that their owners can go to church and confess their prices.

16.   A few years ago we were all blaming petrol for causing air pollution. Now we blame it for causing poverty.

17.   The Government has this great idea for making the roads

safer for pedestrians. They're raising the price of petrol so high that no-one can afford to drive.

18.   Show you how bad things are getting — yesterday I ran out of petrol while driving with my sister.

19.   I didn't realise how much the Arabs were taking over in Britain till I saw the line-up for this year's Derby. It includes three camels.

20.   The price of petrol's got so high even the Arabs can't afford it. The other day I saw two Sheikhs who'd gone back to flying carpets.

There are twenty gags covering a variety of aspects of the subject. We look through them and see which easily link up and lead into each other. It's much the same as piecing a jigsaw puzzle together. Gags 1, 3 and 4 all have a criminal element in them, so they can be linked.

Petrol's so expensive now, yesterday I saw a police car chasing a stolen van and both drivers were out pushing. It's getting that bad that bank robbers are banding together to form carpools. And one bank robber's changed his line altogether. He makes more money mugging smokers for the fuel in their lighters.

There is a possible link between gags 6, 10, 19 and 20.

A few years ago the Germans and Japanese tried to overthrow us by taking our possessions. The Arabs are smarter — they're buying them. I just heard the Saudi Arabians are inviting the British Prime Minister over. They want to meet the person who runs their country. I never realised how big a foothold the Arabs have here until I saw the line-up for this year's Derby. It includes three camels. Mind you, even some Arabs themselves are having trouble keeping up with high oil prices. The other day I heard of two Sheikhs who'd gone back to flying carpets.

The next grouping could be of gags 5, 7, 8, 9, 11 and 18.

Show you how bad things are getting — yesterday I ran out of petrol while driving my sister. But I remember when I

used to go to a garage and tell the attendant, 'Fill her up.'
Now I just say, 'Give me £20's worth.' It's so high, I asked
one garage if they could let me have a pound's worth of petrol
and they just sprayed some behind my ear. If petrol gets any
dearer, I'll have to sell the car to pay for it. I passed one
garage with a notice outside, 'We only charge £1 a gallon.' I
queued up for half an hour before I found that was just for
water. But I should have known what was coming when I
saw the new car owner's handbook. It's got a whole section
on hitchhiking.

That leaves us with gags 2, 12, 13, 14, 15, 16 and 17. To
include 13 would make nonsense of 7, so we'll leave that one out
and see what can be done with the rest.

I remember back to the days when you insured your car to
cover the passengers. Now it's to cover the oil. And remember
when we were all claiming that petrol was the main cause of
air pollution. Now it's something else beginning with P —
poverty. Personally I think it's our government that's behind
this whole oil crisis thing. They're trying to get the
pedestrians' vote. It's a scheme to get the roads safer for
pedestrians by making fuel so expensive none of us can
afford to drive. But the oil companies have to take the blame
too for their profiteering. I don't want to start any rumours,
but I hear that some of them are drilling dry holes on
purpose. They found it's a good place to hide their money.
And some garages have been hiking up their takings too.
That's why a lot of them now close on Sundays. Their owners
are at church confessing their prices. A friend of mine back
from Las Vegas says the filling stations there only charge a
dollar a gallon. That's all they charge, a dollar a gallon. But
to get the petrol, you've got to put a silver dollar in the
pump, pull down the nozzle and be lucky enough to get three
lemons come up.

These wadges of gags easily fit together in almost any order
you like and will make a good four or five minute complete
routine.

*   *   *

Another subject that stand-up comics often talk about is the
crime wave. Here are some random gags on the subject which
we'll try and put into a routine:

26

1. I live in a really tough neighbourhood. The cash register in my local supermarket has a sign, 'Express Lane — for people with six items or a revolver.'

2. Personally I think the Railway Police are the most efficient. I mean, when was the last time you heard of anyone stealing a railway?

3. The criminals are so busy in our neighbourhood you can only get mugged by appointment.

4. I'll say one thing for burglars. They're the only ones where I live that make housecalls.

5. In my neighbourhood, when you work out your weekly budget you have to allow for hold-up money.

6. Crime is really getting out of hand. Yesterday I played a game of Monopoly and someone got murdered in one of my hotels.

7. It's so bad I saw a fellow rob a bank and, on his way to the getaway car, he was mugged.

8. I went to a Weight Watchers' restaurant and while I was watching my weight . . . someone stole my overcoat.

9. I bought a waterbed and found a body at the bottom of it.

10. What we really ought to do is make crime legal . . . and then tax criminals out of business.

11. London's a wonderful place. People come from all over the world to shoplift here.

12. You can tell when you're driving through my district, no one gives hand signals. If they stick their arms out of the car they get their watch nicked.

13. People say nasty things about the Mafia, but they're really polite people. Like I know of one Mafioso who opened the car door for his victim. Mind you, it was going at 70 miles an hour at the time.

14. The police commissioner's taking some definite action

about the increase of muggings in buses and trains. He's going everywhere by taxi.

15.   Last week the police commissioner had a speech prepared on crime . . . and somebody stole it.

16.   We have the only police station I know of that's insured against burglary.

17.   The crime rate's shot up recently. There's now a robbery every two minutes and a mugging every thirty seconds. And that's just in my street.

18.   The kids in our district are in favour of mounted policemen. In fact, the kid next door's got four mounted on his wall.

19.   I know of one veteran criminal who's only fourteen years old. He's too young to drive, so he only steals cars with chauffeurs.

20.   They've got all those concealed cameras in big stores now. There's one shoplifter I know who had to get out of the business altogether because he didn't pass the screen test.

Taking those twenty funny thoughts we'll now dovetail them into each other so they are continuous.

I've just seen the latest crime figures. Did you know there's now a robbery every two minutes and a brutal mugging every thirty seconds? And that's just in my street. It's so bad, I saw a fellow rob a bank and on his way to the getaway car . . . he was mugged. I've never known a time when criminals were so busy. It's ridiculous. Today you have to have an appointment to get mugged.

But, for all that, I still love living in London. It's a great place. It must be. People come from all over the world to shoplift here. The stores have put in those hidden cameras now and they are having some effect. I know of at least two shoplifters who quit the business because they couldn't pass the screen test.

And what are the police doing about it? Well, I hear that last week the police commissioner was going to talk about the fight against crime, but someone stole his speech. But the commissioner has made the first step against crime in the bus and train services. He now goes everywhere by taxi.

A recent survey showed that the Railway Police are the most efficient of all the police services. And that makes sense. After all, when did you last hear of a railway being stolen? Mounted police are getting more prevalent too and my neighbour's kid says he's very keen on mounted police. He's got four of them mounted on the wall of his bedroom. The kid's only fourteen and already a hardened thief. Steals cars. He's too young to drive, so he only steals ones with chauffeurs.

If you're driving through my district you'll know it right away. No one ever gives hand signals. The last one that did had his watch stolen.

Nowhere's safe anymore. I went to a Weight Watchers' restaurant. While I was watching my weight, somebody stole my overcoat. And it's getting harder to work out a weekly budget these days. When you're figuring out how much it costs to live, you never know the amount to set aside for muggings.

Hold-ups are happening everywhere you go. I was in my local supermarket yesterday. They've got a new check-out with a sign, 'Express lane for people with six items or a revolver.'

You'd think the police station would be safe, wouldn't you? But I just found out that even they're insured for burglary. But don't get the idea I'm going to say anything bad against burglars, because I'm not. I mean, they're the only ones we've got left that still make housecalls.

It's those Mafia boys you've got to watch out for. They work in the strangest of places. This morning I was playing Monopoly with my kid and I found a dead body in one of my hotels. It happened to my brother too. He bought himself a waterbed . . . and there was a cemented body in the bottom of it. But from what I hear some of those Mafia boys can be really polite and thoughtful. I know one that even opened the car door for his victim. Mind you, it was driving at 70 miles an hour at the time.

But I've given it a lot of thought and I've come to the conclusion that the only thing to do is to make crime legal. Then tax the criminals out of business like the rest of us.

There are many comedians who specialise in certain subjects or topics. Mort Sahl, David Frost and Ted Rogers do topical political gags. Dave Allen does mostly Irish jokes. Pat Cooper and Gerry Stevens do routines about their Italian backgrounds. Let's stop at this point for a moment and imagine we've been asked to do a routine for Gerry Stevens. Our search for key words to make gags on would go something like this:

We know that so many of the top American singers, like Frank Sinatra, Dean Martin and Tony Bennett, have Italian origins. So the first word on my list would be singers. And Gerry might say:

There's a popular saying that all Italians are good singers. And I can say in all honesty that nobody sang like my Uncle Guido. Mind you, nobody *wanted* to sing like my Uncle Guido! He sounded like a string of spaghetti got loose and was strangling his epiglottis! I've heard voices that were flat before, but this one was horizontal! It was so bad that even deaf people couldn't bear to look at his lips. He once made a recording of that old Trini Lopez song *If I Had a Hammer*. It didn't sell many records, but it sold a lot of hammers. People were buying them to smash the records. Finally he got so bad that the head of the Mafia put out a contract on him. The next day he wound up so full of lead they buried him in the roof.

Italians are mostly Catholics and Catholics are known to have large families. So Gerry might say, 'One thing about us Italians, we always have large families. Ours was so large, when I was a kid our playpen had standing room only.'

Italian women are purported to be plump:

My eldest sister had a definite weight problem, so my mother put her on the water diet. Two days a week nothing but water passed her lips. In the first week she lost twelve pounds, but she gained five gallons.

My sister was far from good looking. She had one of those faces that stretches mother-love to the limit. Other girls, when they go out at night, carry a whistle or a cosh for protection in case a man starts with them. Not my sister. All she carried was a torch. If a man came near her she just shone it on her face.

Italian women are famous for being emotional. And my mother's typically Italian that way. The most emotional woman I know. I went home the other day and there was my mother sitting on the couch in the living room crying her eyes out. She was sobbing like mad. And there was my father, leaning over her saying, 'For goodness sake, Rosa, it's only a commercial. He comes back to her after she's cleaned her teeth.'

Italian girls are very romantic and my family think I made a big mistake in not marrying an Italian girl. But my wife *is* very romantic. For instance, when I came home from work last night she was in a very romantic mood. I knew it because she had a twinkle in her eye . . . her shoulder strap was dangling seductively . . . and she was hugging and kissing the milkman!

Italy has the worst pollution problem in the world, but the Mafia have told the Government they're going to help clean it up. They're only going to dump half as many bodies in the river this year.

Italians are big eaters:

When our family got together for Christmas dinner last December it was like a battlefield. As soon as they saw the turkey everyone made a grab. Hands were grabbing for the legs . . . other hands for the breasts . . . and about a dozen other hands for the drumsticks. In two seconds the whole turkey was completely eaten. But Mum didn't mind. Saved her cooking it.

But in an Italian house at mealtimes all you hear is *pasta*. 'Pasta salt . . . pasta pepper . . . pasta bicarbonate of soda!' My family were such big eaters. They'd eat anything. After every meal we had to make a head count to make sure we were all still there.

Those are just a few example gags that you could do on the subject of having an Italian family. There are, of course, the inevitable standards like: 'My mother was the nearest thing you could imagine to Sophia Loren. She looked like Carlo Ponti.' Or: 'People think of Al Capone as a gangster, but to me, he'll always be thought of as a lover. I mean, he never ever forgot Valentine's Day.'

British comic Les Dawson, in his monologues, has a 'smirking' delivery. He gives the impression that he is long suffering and always hard-done-by. If you take his gags apart you'll find that the main ingredient is exaggeration. He claims to have the fattest of mother-in-laws.

She's so fat, when she was on jury duty the other eleven had to wait outside.

She's so fat, one night a bandleader dedicated a number to her. He played 'Sixteen Tons' twice.

She's so fat, she doesn't have measurements — she has time zones.

She's so fat, everytime she shivers the seismograph at Greenwich registers an earthquake.

She's so fat, she has to put on a corset before she can put on her corset.

She's so fat, the pilot always makes her get off the plane first. Then they can take off.

I'll never forget the day I met her. She was the first one to break the ice. We were at a skating rink at the time.

No wonder she's so fat. For breakfast she eats more than I weigh.

While we're talking about fat gags, let's reverse the situation and imagine that we are asked to write a routine for a fat comedian. I myself would adopt the American approach of making the comedian big-headed. In other words, I'd have him praising himself and considering himself to be sexually attractive. He might start off by saying:

Good evening. Don't worry, ladies, I won't stay out here long. I know that a body as sexy as mine must be too much for some of you to bear. But please, control yourselves. There's enough of me for all of you.

They wanted me for the centrefold of *Cosmopolitan* Magazine . . . nude. Well, why not? I say if you've got something worth showing — show it! I spent all day posing for the picture . . . with a hand covering my most intimate parts. It was great fun. Especially as it wasn't my hand.

When I got the letter with the offer to pose I immediately told my wife. I said, 'Darling, guess who's begging me to let them publish a nude picture of me?' She said, 'That's easy. *Mad* Magazine.' I said, 'No, *Cosmopolitan*.' She said, 'Oh, that would be in answer to my request. I told them it was about time they had something funny.'

I said, 'Don't laugh at my figure. I have the same weight

and measurements as John Wayne had.' She said, 'Yes. Till he got off his horse.'

She should talk. She's built like a rake. You should see her undressed. Two more belly buttons and she could be mistaken for a flute. She sent me to buy a bra for her the other day. The salesgirl said, 'What size cup?' I said, 'What are you talking about — cup? She hasn't even got enough for a wine glass.'

I never understood what all the fuss was about when women started going topless. My wife's gone topless for years, only nobody noticed. Skinniness runs in her family. They once lined up her family for a group picture. They looked like the railings outside Buckingham Palace.

She tried to force me to get skinny too. Only cooked non-fattening food. Roast breast of radish. Stuffed grapes. And for dessert — skimmed prune juice. After two weeks you wouldn't recognise me. I wasted away to an elephant.

There are all sorts of directions you can go from there. Talking about health . . . about marriage . . . about clothes . . . just about anything. But the point I was trying to get across is that if your comedian is fat, don't ignore it. Make use of it. Joke about it. It puts the audience at ease and establishes a good link between them and the performer.

Schnozzle Durante got laughs by saying: 'With my nose, amongst the Eskimos I'm known as Casanova.' Or: 'With my nose I have to use a bed sheet for a handkerchief. And a second bed sheet for the other nostril.' Or: 'With my size nose, every time I face the audience the first four rows have to duck.' If a comedian with a normal size schnoz said those lines they wouldn't mean a thing. They'd been 'tailored' to fit the individual peculiarities of Mr Durante.

Mickey Rooney could get a laugh with 'I'm so small I have to kneel down to comb my hair.' Conversely, Steve Allen could say, 'I'm so tall I have to stand up to comb my hair.' But these lines only work because Rooney is just five foot tall and Allen is six foot three. However, it's an interesting point to show how the same gag can so easily be switched for opposite circumstances.

If your comedian has anything physically different about him, play on it for laughs. There is a very good British comedian who works in a wheelchair. A typical gag from his act is: 'I went to Lourdes and a miracle happened. I got two new tyres.'

Comedy actress Diana Dors always opened her act with a specially written song which made fun of her bleached hair, her much over-publicised sex life and just about everything else the press had said to ridicule her. It worked well because it not only gave the impression of humility, but it definitely broke down any barrier of embarrassment that may have impaired the good and necessary relationship between Miss Dors and her audience.

Perry Como used the same approach by opening his performance with a song written for him that laughs at his completely grey hair and his supposed laziness. 'I make a point of taking a nap 40 minutes before a show and don't wake up till the show's over.' Como is clever to point out to his audience that his hair *is* grey and that he is starting to look his real age. They'll be seeing this for themselves anyway. So it's best to show your audience that you know your own defects and can even laugh at them yourself. They are, in fact, invaluable props to hang the comedy on.

Another important thing to remember when building a comedian's act is to try and include the audience in the comedy. Almost make them part of it. This is done quite simply by making the comedy, where possible, conversational. Let me give you an illustration of what I mean. Your comedian could say, 'We were so poor in our family that my father married off my sisters just for the rice.' Or he could involve the audience by putting the same gag this way: 'I bet a lot of you come from a family as poor as mine was. And you probably remember how, during the depression, your father got your sisters married off just for the rice.'

Suppose the new comedian you've found doesn't have a recognisable physical characteristic. What do you do then? Well, you could probably create one for him. Perhaps you could do something about his way of standing. Veteran American comic, Jack Durante, used to dance on stage, bypass the microphone and fall straight into the orchestra pit. Then he'd climb back on stage and be so physically shot that he'd have to hold on to the mike stand with both hands for support. A unique stance. And because he was out of breath, his gag delivery was unique too. His opening line was: 'You are now looking at the image of a married man. This morning my wife said to me, "Jack, you'll drive me to my grave." I had the car out in two minutes!' He always gave the impression of just managing to get the punchline out before running out of breath. It was clever timing. Jack Durante's own individual style.

Groucho Marx invented his famous stooped walk and painted-on false moustache. He completed his characterisation with that unlit cigar. They were his trademarks. Just as Jack Benny's toupee was. Benny had a full growth of natural hair, but by 'inventing' the story of his wearing a toupee he was able to create a whole new area for his comedy. You'd hear Benny say, 'Rochester, I can't remember, have I had my haircut this month?' And Rochester would reply, 'Not yet, Boss. It's down at the Barber Shop right now!'

Have you noticed the way George Burns times his laughs with his cigar? When he sticks it in his mouth you know the gag is finished and he doesn't take it out again until the laughter has subsided and he's ready to start the next gag. Phyllis Diller shrieks with laughter at the end of each one of her one-liners. She's out to give the impression that she thinks that what she's said is funny too. Many comedians do this. It's called 'laughing home the gag'. It's usually done with a gag or joke that the comedian himself isn't too sure of and so he 'laughs it home' to show that it is supposed to be funny.

It's an old Show Business trick to do a 'planned break-up' or 'planned dry' in which the comedian pretends that something unexpected has happened, or that he has forgotten his next punchline. He laughs and ad libs funnier lines, and the audience laugh louder with him thinking they are experiencing something unprepared. It's the same thing as them catching the comedian with his pants down.

Johnny Carson's staff of six comedy writers prepare some great gags for those opening monologues in his *Tonight Show*. But more often than not he will deliver them with what appears to be a lack of enthusiasm. This is so he can score heavily with his lines about how bad the gags are. We're led to believe his lines are ad lib but I doubt that more than just the odd few are. That's Carson's gimmick, the ad lib 'savers'.

One of the most important questions you have to ask yourself when writing for a comedian is, 'Is he a funny man? Or is he just a good performer who can put over a funny script?' This enables you to observe one of the cardinal rules of comedy writing. That is, to have a straight man doing funny things, or a funny man doing straight things, but never the opposite way round.

Of course, some writers and comedians have bent this rule and got away with it, but generally the rule should be obeyed to get the best results.

You see, believability is an important factor in true comedy. If a comedian is funny in himself then all the writer has to do is put him in a normal situation and his reactions to that situation will be funny. He will, because he thinks funny and in a different way from normal people, misconstrue the situation and act according to his own interpretation of it. The technique of creating and writing these situations is dealt with in full later when we discuss the plotting and characterisations in situation comedy.

What I'm trying to make clear to you here is that when you try to put a funny man in a funny situation you are weakening the comedy potential of both. When you first learned grammar at school they taught you that two negatives make a positive. In other words, they cancel each other out. It's the same basic rule in comedy.

Perhaps you are not yet sure how we classify the difference between a funny man and a normal comedian. A funny man is funny because he's peculiar in some way. He has an attitude to life that makes him act and react in a different way to other people. He could be the perennial drunk like Foster Brooks, or the Poor Souls that Charlie Chaplin and Harry Langdon were, or the parsimonious tightwad that Jack Benny was. You can name many more yourself. They'll be people like Woody Allen, who sees himself as a complete nonentity, or Don Knotts, who's so nervous he can't say one complete sentence without getting it wrong.

When writing for a funny man the writer has to think up, concoct, contrive or whatever you want to call it, a situation that highlights that performer's funny peculiarities. The system of writing for this kind of performer is that, having dreamt up the situation, you close your eyes and imagine yourself to be that person in that situation. And then you write down what that person would do faced with that situation. That's how you get your routine.

The 'normal' comedian is a guy (or gal) who needs a script to be funny. That's a *script* as against a *situation*.

It might help to clarify this if I sub-divide normal comedians into two classes. Class one would have people like Ted Rogers, Jimmy Tarbuck, Bob Monkhouse, Mike Reid, Roy Walker, Henny Youngman, Myron Cohen, Joey Bishop, Corbett Monica and that kind of stand-up comic. They're funny if the gags or jokes they're telling you are funny. Usually they are and so all of them have been earning a regular living.

But my second classification would include comedians like Tom O'Connor, Dave Allen, Frankie Howerd, Michael Bentine, Jasper Carrott, Shelley Berman, Alan King, Jackie Mason, Milt Kamen, Bill Cosby and Rodney Dangerfield. These are all guys who do set routines. Not just a string of gags or jokes. They talk about a subject as though they were having a friendly chat rather than performer and audience.

Alan King is a good example. His style is one of self-identification. He's been through all the same problems as his audience. With their wives, their disrespectful kids, with non-obliging taxi drivers and with over-officious bureaucrats. He relates his experiences (his comedy routines) just as though he was talking to us across the room at a party. We're fellow sufferers and most of the time what we're really doing is laughing at ourselves.

There are probably thousands of nightclub comics telling jokes about their wives. But we know they are jokes. However, when Alan King tells us the same things about his wife, we believe him.

We can see him actually suffering through it as he acts out his stories. And right there is the basic ingredient for the recipe that makes a top comedian. He's an actor. I've always contended that if you found a performer who really knows the craft of acting, you could provide the right material and make him or her a comic.

You'll find most of Alan King's best routines in the two books he's had published. They're called *Help! I'm a Prisoner in a Chinese Bakery* and *Anyone Who Owns His Own Home Deserves It*. Both are available in paperback from Avon Books, 959 Eighth Avenue, New York, N.Y. 10019. Or you might be able to borrow a copy from your local library.

Rodney Dangerfield's style is one I particularly like. He calls himself 'The Loser'. That, in fact, is the title of the first of his three comedy LPs. His catchphrase, 'I don't get no respect', sums up the kind of character he portrays in his monologues. Rodney's the kind of guy who, when he opens a Christmas cracker, finds a parking ticket inside. Who buys his wife a new hat and then gets stuck for matching gloves, handbag and shoes. Who buys a waterproof watch just before a drought. Who pays five hundred dollars for a burglar alarm system and the same night his place burns down.

Dangerfield's gimmick is that nothing works right for him. He is continually putting himself down. Here are examples of the kind of gag he's famous for.

I told my psychiatrist that nobody likes me. He said I was being ridiculous — everyone hasn't met me yet.

As a kid I had a lot of charisma. Then I started dating girls and my charisma cleared up.

I was once about to make love to the Bionic Woman and her battery broke down.

When I was engaged to my wife I wanted a big wedding — and she wanted to call the whole thing off.

I told my wife the truth. I told her I was seeing a psychiatrist. Then she told me the truth. That's she's seeing a psychiatrist, two plumbers and a bartender.

My wife and I sleep in separate rooms, have dinner apart and take separate vacations. We think a couple should do everything they can to keep their marriage together.

Phyllis Diller too, relies on a self-deprecating style to win warmth and laughter from her audience. The subjects she chooses are her supposed ugliness, her poor sense of fashion, her misshapen figure, her failure as a housewife, her husband 'Fang''s drink problem and laziness and her general frustration at not being a sex symbol. Typical Diller gags are:

I'm worried about sexual harrassment. Nobody bothers me.

My health is not bad. Thank God I feel better than I look.

I'm only in Show Business part time. My main income's from renting myself out for Halloween parties.

I've had my body lifted so many times my navel is now the cleft in my chin.

My photos do me an injustice. They look just like me.

The closest I've come to suicide is marriage.

I've been asked to say a couple of words about my husband Fang. How about short and cheap?

To Fang a good year for whisky is the year he drinks it!

Fang has that lean look. Everytime I look at him he's leaning on something.

Dean Martin, no mean comic in his own right, also has an

identification in his humour. That of being an alcoholic. Martin's funniest gags are along these lines:

Actually it only takes one drink to get me loaded. Trouble is I can't remember whether it's the thirteenth or fourteenth.

The doctor said if I didn't stop drinking I'd lose my hearing. I told him, the stuff I'm drinking's a lot better than the stuff I've been hearing.

I'm grateful to my family because they give me a lot of support. Mainly on the way home from parties.

I always go to sleep feeling great and wake up in the morning with a hangover. I'm beginning to think it's not the drink . . . it's the sleep that does it.

Woody Allen is the timid little guy who enjoys talking about his troubles.

When I was born my mother was terribly disappointed. Not that she wanted a girl. She wanted a divorce.

I'm one of those people that's not afraid to die. I just don't want to be there when it happens.

I can take care of myself. In case of danger I have this cutlass that I carry around with me. And if there's a real emergency I press the handle and it turns into a white cane so I can get sympathy.

I keep having this birthday cake fantasy, where they wheel out a big cake with a girl in it, and she pops out and hurts me and gets back in.

After six years of marriage my wife and I pondered whether to take a vacation or get a divorce . . . and we decided that a trip to Bermuda is over in two weeks, but a divorce is something you always have.

The problem with my wife was her immaturity. I'd be in the bathroom taking a bath and she would walk right in and sink my boats.

George Burns has outlasted most of his contemporaries and uses his longevity as his gimmick.

I had a record at number one. That wasn't the chart placing, it was the serial number, I made it that long ago.

I have my 87th birthday coming up and people ask what I'd most appreciate getting. I'll tell you. A paternity suit.

I'm going around with a young girl now, but I'm not kidding myself about it. I know she's only after me for my body.

I'm at that age now where just putting my cigar in its holder is a thrill.

Bob Hope is an interesting case because most of his gags are hard and aimed at the vulnerabilities of other people. But they are nevertheless acceptable because he also highlights his own weaknesses.

Dean Martin is the most relaxed performer on television. He never spills a word.

Phyllis Diller's had so many facelifts there's nothing left in her shoes.

Zsa Zsa Gabor got married as a one off and it was so successful she turned it into a series.

Jackie Gleason's so fat he was born on July 2nd, and 3rd. If he'd been born today they'd have had to get Dolly Parton in to breastfeed him.

In Russia they treated me like a Czar — and you know how they treated the Czar.

I asked the priest if I'd be committing a sin if I played golf on the Sabbath. He said the way I play it's a sin any day.

I told my music teacher I'd been brushing up on my singing. He heard my voice and said I must have been using a wire brush.

You should now have a fairly good idea of the various styles used by top comedians and know how to routine gags for them.

3 / Sketches, Quickies, Black-Outs and Cross-Overs

Quite often new writers send in quickies which they erroneously label as sketches. Although there are no hard and fast rules laid down about this, a sketch usually lasts for two minutes or more. Under two minutes, it's a miniature sketch and is called a *quickie*. Here are examples of quickies:*

* In Chapter 8 I'll talk about how you should set out a script to send to a producer or script editor.

The Set: Wall of a Desert Fort. Day.

A Legionnaire Captain is addressing a Legionnaire Private who is standing to attention.

Captain: So, Legionnaire, you still insist on going on this suicide patrol?
Private: Yes, mon Capitan.
Captain: If you're captured, you know what the dreaded El Hamid does to his prisoners?
Private: Yes, mon Capitan.
Captain: And you're volunteering of your own free will?
Private: Yes, mon Capitan.
Captain: I must ask you — why are you doing this?
Private: Because, mon Capitan — I want to get on!

* * *

The Set: Interior of a Bank. Day.

A woman Teller is behind the counter. She is finishing serving a man and immediately behind him in the queue is a furtive looking Robber. It's the Robber's turn as he steps up to the counter.

Teller: Yes, sir?
Robber: (Whispers) This is a stick-up. Hand over all your money. I've got a bomb in my pocket set to go off in just thirty seconds.
Teller: I'm sorry, you're mumbling, sir. Would you speak a little louder?
Robber: (Whispers a little louder) I said I've got a bomb in my pocket, and if you don't hand it all over . . . it'll go off right here.
Teller: I still can't hear you, sir. You really must speak louder.
Robber: (Impatient. Whispers louder) I said, hand over all your money. I've got this bomb . . .

At this point he holds up the bomb device to show her. It explodes. We hear a loud bang and there's a puff of smoke to simulate the explosion.

When the smoke clears, the Robber's clothes are tattered and torn and his face dirty with smoke.

Robber: Forget it. The service here was *always* too slow!

* * *

The Set: Boxer's Dressing Room.   Night.

The Boxer is wearing a dressing gown with the name 'Killer McCoy' on the back. He is in a passionate embrace with a young lady.

The door bursts open and the young lady's Father enters angrily. They see him and immediately break apart from the embrace.

Girl: Dad!
Father: (Angry) Yes, my girl, I thought I'd find you here! I've warned you about this before! No daughter of mine is going to be alone in the dressing room with Killer McCoy!
Girl: But Dad, I'm twenty-one. I'm a big girl now.
Father: That's got nothing to do with it.
Girl: But I'm able to take care of myself.
Father: I don't care. I'm still not allowing you to be in here with him!
Girl: But why, Dad? Give me one good reason?
Father: I'll give you a very good reason. I'm his trainer!

End with Father taking off his jacket and we see the jersey he's wearing underneath has the Boxer's name on it.

These quickies would run somewhere between thirty seconds and a minute, depending on the way the director shoots them. It is essential that all quickies have a definite end to them. Tags or punch-lines, as they are called. If you can continue the story beyond the tag or punch-line then you haven't written a proper quickie. It would be just an illustrated gag. For instance:

The Set: A Courtroom.   Day.

Prosecuting Counsel is about to question the very attractive young lady in the stand.

Counsel: Miss Goodbody, I have just three simple questions to put to you. The first is, what were you doing on the night of January the fourth? Second, what were you doing on the night of March the sixth? And thirdly, and most important of all, what are you doing tonight?

That's a gag that fits in well if you're writing a courtroom sketch, but is not a miniature sketch on its own and therefore not a quickie.

Another important thing about writing quickies, which a lot of new writers overlook, is the expense of production. They write them for large casts and often with several sets or expensive filming. One editor says someone sent him this one in:

Set: Psychiatrist's Consulting Room.   Day.

The Psychiatrist is behind his desk. His female receptionist enters.

Receptionist: Doctor, there's a man outside who thinks he's Napoleon.
Doctor: (Annoyed) Oh, not another one. Tell him to go away.
Receptionist: I did, Doctor. But he wants to know what to do with *them*.

She points out of the window. The Psychiatrist looks out of the window. Camera shoots through window and we see a long winding trail of French Soldiers in uniforms of the Napoleonic era with a man dressed as Napoleon at the head of them.

He thought it was a very funny gag. And I did too. But the hiring of all those men to play the soldiers and also uniforms for them would blow the show's whole budget for one fifteen-second quickie. It just isn't practical. And the reason successful writers become so successful is that what they write is not just funny, but practical too.

The most successful of today's comedy writers carefully consider the number of characters and sets (pieces of scenery) they use.

That's why they are doing so well. Their scripts are easy to produce.

It's not difficult to think of gags that require lots of scenery and need to be filmed from a helicopter. But no matter how funny they are your chances of selling them are small. The producer must consider his budget limitations. And if you want to sell him a quickie, *you* must consider this too.

Most shows that use quickies will let it be known to writers whether they have facilities for filming. Not all shows have this expensive luxury. And, of course, filming is not always possible in bad weather or poor light. Often the producer will have chosen certain locations for his filming and will ask for quickies that will fit in with those locations. He might be going to Knottsbury Park and will therefore require cowboy quickies. Or he may be going to Disneyland and ask for quickies using Disney characters. Perhaps he's going to a circus, funfair, airport, hospital, railway station or on board an ocean liner.

Possibly a producer will request quickies on a subject or theme for a particular show. Let's take crime again as the given subject. Robbery comes under that heading. Here's a quickie on an attempted robbery at a bank:

The Set: Interior of a Bank. Day.

A Bank Teller is behind his counter filling up a small sack with money.

Robber is on the Customer's side of the counter pointing a pistol threateningly at him.

Robber: Come on, hurry it up! I haven't got all day!

Robber's Wife enters. She sees him standing there.

Wife: So there you are. I've been looking all over for you.
Robber: (Annoyed) I've told you a hundred times, Alice, never interrupt me when I'm working!
Wife: If it were just for me, I wouldn't. But it's our little son, Johnny. He's at home crying his eyes out.
Robber: Why? Is he ill?

Wife: No, but you took his water pistol by mistake!

Robber reacts with a foolish look on his face.

Robber: (To Teller) Hold the order, I'll be back later.

He exits cursing his luck.

A further quickie in the same set could be considered as a switch on the one with the bomb.

The Set.   Interior of a Bank.   Day.

Robber enters and goes to counter where a Teller is free to serve him.

Teller: Yes sir, can I help you?
Robber: Hand over your money! I've got a gun in my pocket.
Teller: Oh yes? That's what they all say. I don't believe you.
Robber: I have. I've got this gun in my pocket.

Robber tries to get the pistol out of his pocket to show the Teller, but it is stuck there. He keeps struggling to pull it from his pocket but with no success.

Teller: I still don't believe you.
Robber: (Getting annoyed) I have. I tell you I definitely have this gun in my pocket. I'll show it to you as soon as I can get it out.

He continues to pull at the gun.

Robber: (To Teller) Just hold on a minute.

Struggles further.

Robber: Won't be long now.

Another Customer has come in and lined up behind the Robber.

47

Robber: (To Teller) Serve this gentleman first.

Robber lets the other man go up to the counter, but while he is being served the camera stays on the Robber still tugging hard to extract the pistol from his pocket.

Robber: (Pleased) It's coming! It's coming!

Then, as he makes one final pull at the gun inside his pocket, it goes off.

F/X.   A Gunshot.

Robber: (To Teller) Leave it for now . . . I'll come back tomorrow. *(Limping off — having shot himself in the foot)* Which way to the hospital?

Here are two quickies that too are economical to produce because they use the same set. The first deals with a complaint of assault and the second is someone phoning in for help.

Set: Reception Area of Police Station.   Day.

A middle-aged Woman rushes in. She is very excited. Her coat is torn and her hat is almost falling off her head.

Woman: (Hysterical) Police! Police! I want the police!
Police Sergeant: Yes Madam, can I be of assistance?
Woman: Yes, you've got to help me! I was just walking in the park when a man jumped out of the bushes without warning . . . and he kissed me and hugged me . . . and dragged me into the woods!
Police Sergeant: And you want us to find this man?
Woman: Yes. *(Very eager)* And tell him I'm free all day tomorrow!

Fade out on her eager smile.

* * *

Set: Reception area of Police Station. Day.

Police Sergeant is speaking into the phone. We merely hear the man's voice at the other end of the phone, not see him.

Police Sergeant: (To phone) I'm sorry sir, I didn't hear that. Would you mind saying it again?

Man's Voice: Please, this is very urgent! I think I am about to be shot by my very jealous wife.

Police Sergeant: (To phone) I see sir, and have you any particular reason for thinking that?

Man's Voice: Yes — she's standing right in front of me here, holding a loaded revolver. Please do something!

Police Sergeant: (To phone) Don't worry sir, I'll be right over. Just where are you?

Man's Voice: I'm at two hundred and forty six B, Cassiobury Park Avenue.

Police Sergeant: (To phone) I'll just write that down, sir. You said two hundred and forty six Cassenbury Avenue . . .

Man's Voice: No. Two hundred and forty six *B*, and it's Cassiobury Park Avenue. Cassiobury, not Cassenbury.

Police Sergeant: (To phone) Cassiobury? I don't know that one. How do you spell it?

Man's Voice: (More panic) For God's sake! It's C-A-S-S-I-O-B-U-R-Y. And please, do get a move on. She's cocked the trigger.

Police Sergeant: (To phone) It's all right sir, it's all in hand. I'll just look it up in my street guide.

Policeman rests phone on the counter and picks up street guide book and starts to thumb through it looking for the right page.

Over the phone we hear a pistol shot. A mild scream from the man and then a thud as his body hits the floor.

Police Sergeant picks up the phone again.

Police Sergeant: (To phone) Hello! Hello, sir! *(There is naturally no answer)* Oh, what a shame. *(Putting phone down)* If he'd lived in the High Street, I could have saved him!

49

Continuing with the crime theme we'll move on to the police shoot-out which was a regular feature of all the old gangster films. Having these take place at night makes them a lot easier to produce. All we need is the front of a house in the studio with a searchlight shone on it.

The Set.   Exterior Street.   Night.

Two policemen with guns kneeling beside what suggests to be a car. It's a shoot-out. The Chief of Police picks up a megaphone and shouts through it towards the house.

Police Chief: (Shouting) You may as well give up, Johnson, we've got the place surrounded. If you know what's good for you you'll throw out your weapons and come out with your hands above your head.
Johnson: (Voice only) OK, Copper, you win.

In slow succession there's a whole armoury of weapons thrown out of the window. Pistols, knives, swords, shotguns, rifles, bazookas and finally a machine gun.

Johnson: (Voice only) I'm coming out myself now.

Johnson emerges from the front door of the house with his hands on top of his head.

Police Chief puts handcuffs on him.

Police Chief: OK, Johnson, I'm booking you. And *(Pointing to the collection of weapons on the ground)* I've got the evidence right here.
Johnson: What's the charge?
Police Chief: Littering the pavement!

Fade on them taking the Crook off.

*   *   *

The Set.   Exterior Street.   Night.

A Crook (Rocky) is holed up in the house shooting it out with the Police.

We hear the crash of a window and pistol shots being fired from inside of it.

There are several uniformed Police in the foreground shooting back at the window.

Police Chief: Hand me the megaphone. *(Shouts through megaphone)* You'd better surrender, Rocky, you ain't got a chance!
Rocky: (Voice only) That's what you think, Copper. I've got enough ammunition here to kill the lot of you.

There are two more volleys of gunfire from both directions.

Police Chief: (To his own men) Hold your fire, I've just had a thought. *(Shouts through megaphone)* Hey Rocky, let's have a truce for a minute. I want to talk to you.
Rocky: OK, Copper, but I'm warning you, don't try anything.

Police Chief crosses to broken window.

Rocky: What do you want, Hannigan?
Police Chief: Do you have a licence for that gun in your hand?
Rocky: Yeah.
Police Chief: Let me see it.

Rocky shows him a slip of paper which he studies carefully and then returns to him.

Police Chief: Yeah, that seems in order. Ah well, it was just a thought.

Police Chief returns to his men.

Police Chief: OK men, carry on firing.

The Police fire shots.

Police Chief: (Through megaphone) You'd better give up, Rocky. You ain't got a chance.

End on both sides firing just as we started.

All the quickies I have shown you so far have had a verbal content. But some of the best ones are silent. Here are three which were written by former students of mine which I was able to buy when I was script editor for a BBC Television series.

Dutch Boy Quickie   by Bob Shaw

The Set: A Dyke in Holland

A spout of water is coming through a small hole in the dyke. A small boy enters wearing period Dutch costume.

He sees the water coming through and stands there pondering what to do for a few seconds. Then his face lights up as an idea strikes him.

He sticks his finger in the hole and stops the water coming through. But a second later the water starts to spout out through both his ears. (Note: The appearance of water coming out of his ears is done by a trick effect.)

*　　*　　*

Man Taking a Shower Quickie by Manny Curtis

The Set.   Exterior.   A wall background.

We see a man from waist up with water pouring down on him as from a shower. He is apparently naked and is singing to himself while scrubbing his back with a long handled brush.

After establishing this shot for a few seconds the camera pulls out slowly to reveal the man is wearing just swimming trunks and is standing in an open topped car in a car wash.

*　　*　　*

Golfer Quickie   by Les Higgins

The Set.   A Golf Course.

The Golfer takes a club out of his golf bag and gets into a proper golfing stance.

He looks away up the fairway as if lining up his shot. Then, after a couple of practice swings, he takes a proper swing.

Then he bends down and picks up a boiled egg, the top of which he has just sliced off. He takes a spoon out of his pocket and starts to eat the egg as we fade the picture.

By now you should have a pretty good idea of what constitutes a quickie and also the simplest way to set them out on paper. Script editors insist that you only put one quickie on each sheet of paper and that your full name and address is on every one.

From the examples I've shown you, you should now be able to pick your own subjects and have a crack at writing some. Now let's move on to *black-outs:*

Again, it's probably best to show what these are by giving examples.

Set: Anywhere.   Anytime.

A young man and young woman are together.

She: I took this engagement ring you gave me to the jeweller to have it valued. He told me it's only an *imitation* diamond.
He: I know. You keep telling me to save the real thing till after we're married!

Lights are blacked out

* * *

Set: Forest clearing.   Day.

Three Macbeth witches around the boiling cauldron.

53

First Witch: Bats eyes and frogs tails!
2nd Witch: Lizards arms and spiders toes!
3rd Witch: Hmmmmm . . . Sounds delicious. What's for dessert?

Lights are blacked out

* * *

Set.   An Office.   Day.

Boss addresses his Secretary.

Boss: Miss Benson, what have you done with all my computer cards?
Secretary: I threw them away. Well, they were full of holes!

Lights are blacked out

If you're trying to sell black-outs it's usually helpful to have batches of six using the same set and characters so they can all be recorded at the same time and used as a running gag throughout the show or series.

Dave Allen, for instance, would have recorded most of his confessional black-outs at the one time. After all, they all used the same set and he didn't have to keep changing into that same priest's costume. Costume changes during the recording of a show are a big problem. That's why a recorded show is very often shot out of sequence. The comedian will do his closing speech at the same time as his opening speech to save him changing back into his tuxedo from whatever costume he wore in the last sketch or production number.

* * *

Cross-overs were a kind of gag pioneered by the old Minstrel shows, and they became the stock-in-trade of most of the old time double acts. You must have seen it a thousand times where the straight man would be talking or singing when the comedian would walk across stage carrying some luggage. The straight man stops and asks, 'What do you think you're doing?' And the comic replies, 'I'm taking my case to court,' and goes off. A few seconds later he'd be back with a ladder and explain that he was going to a higher court. They were gags done as the comic crosses over the stage and so became known as cross-overs. Often they're done without any props and are just an excuse to get in a riddle. The straight man would be talking when the comic would come on and say, 'I say, I say, I say! What did the doctor say to the man who thought he was a pack of cards?' 'I don't know. What *did* the doctor say to the man who thought he was a pack of cards?' 'He said, "I'll deal with you later!"' And then he'd (very wisely) go off.

There's very little call for cross-overs these days though *Laugh-In* did start a revival of them not too long ago.

So far I've explained the difference between cross-overs, blackouts, quickies and sketches. Now I'd like to carry on with just *sketches*:

There are probably as many forms of sketches as there are gags. As in Chapter One, we'll list some of them to show the kind of variation you can get into any sketch show you may be asked to write for:

1. **The Send-Up or Parody** This is where you take a well known film or play or TV Show and make fun of it. Don't keep too accurately to the original story. That may be dangerous and get you a lawsuit for plagiarism or infringement of copyright. Just use the general idea. I've never actually seen a James Bond film, but I've sold eight very successful sketches which were parodies of James Bond.

Johnny Carson did a funny sketch called *Canine v. Canine* which was a parody on the Dustin Hoffman film *Kramer v. Kramer*. In the Carson version it was two dogs, after their divorce, contesting the custody of their puppy.

These sketches work well because the audience already know the characters and characteristics that you are poking fun at.

2. **The Situation** This is a much shorter version of a situation comedy show. But you have to start, develop and end the story within the time and budget confines of a sketch. With sketches you are usually restricted to just one set and expected to keep down the number of characters used, too.

One situation sketch I wrote had the comic buy a book on salesmanship and get himself a job as a commercial traveller selling soap. He went to sell soap to the owner of a hardware shop. The owner, a much better and more experienced salesman, didn't buy the soap but twisted the comic's words back against him and managed to sell him almost everything in the shop.

In another situation I had a different comedian preparing for his girlfriend to come round for the evening. Just as she arrived, he sneezed and broke his trouser belt. He had to go through serving her with food and drinks and even dancing with her without his trousers falling down . . . and without her knowing they were in danger of falling down. When he fixed a broken light switch with one hand, the other holding his trousers up, she asked, 'If you used two hands would you get a shock?' He replied, 'No, but *you* might.'

Another situation sketch had the comedian's car break down near the country cottage of a friend. He decided to stop over there for the night. But unbeknown to him, the friend had sold the cottage to a young lady. The set was a main room with a bed that pulled down from the wall. One door led off to the unseen kitchen and the other to a small bathroom. The comedian made several trips back and forth to the bathroom to clean his teeth, wash his socks, shave, etc. And the girl kept making trips to the kitchen to check the meal she was cooking. Neither was in the main room at the same time as the other. When either the man or the girl re-entered the room something would have either been moved or removed by the other and they suspected ghosts. It was a situation easily exploited for laughs because the audience knew something that neither the comedian or the girl knew.

3. **The Play on Words** This type of sketch is where the laughs come because you transpose the vernacular of a trade, profession, sport or whatever and have the characters talking like that in an alien situation. In a regular TV revue type series I had the lead male and female performers do a love scene each week as different characters. One week they'd be cinema ushers, the next week shop stewards, then police officers, doctors, Olympic athletes, stackers in supermarkets, football fans, etc. The situation never changed, but the dialogue was the kind spoken by the people in those trades, professions or vocations.

4. **The Domestic** This again could be a capsulated version of a situation comedy. The difference here is that the premise of the sketch is built round the home and family. It's usually a husband and wife situation. Or perhaps they have some guests in the house.

A situation where the husband has brought his boss home unexpectedly for supper and the wife is angry because she is unprepared . . . That's an oft used basis for a typical domestic sketch.

Or the domestic sketch could be something much more simple

like a husband and wife arguing over whether their son should be taught sex at school or if it's the father's duty to do it. I got a very funny four minutes out of this premise for one of my shows in Holland.

Another domestic situation might have the wife so enthused with her new interest of yoga that she insists on her husband partaking in it too. Against his will he is forced to eat and watch TV in yoga positions. His food is mostly vegetarian from yoga books. And when he wants to talk with his wife, or complain about things, she won't listen because she's meditating. If the man is depicted as a typical New York manual labourer you will have the nucleus of a good sketch here.

5. **Mistaken Identity** The old example given of this is the one where a man wants to sell his baby car and the buyer thinks he just wants to sell his baby. Laughs come out of the buyer's reaction to such lines as, 'She leaks badly. Every time she stands still for any time, there's a pool on the floor.' 'I make sure she's kept clean. Once a week I take her out in the back yard and hose her down.' 'If I can't sell her, I'll just abandon her on the street somewhere'.

This is probably the simplest form of sketch to write. There are many variations on it. I did one for comic magician Tommy Cooper when he arrived in New York to appear on the *Ed Sullivan Show*. Boxer Henry Cooper also arrived that day for a fight in Madison Square Garden. In my sketch Tommy is mistaken by a taxi driver for Henry and taken to the Garden. He thinks he is at the TV Studios and much fun was got out of his surprise at the stiff medical test and the way they dressed him in shorts and bandaged his hands before going on to do his magic act. He assumed they were bandaging his hands to make his conjuring tricks harder. And that they'd stripped him to the waist so he couldn't hide anything up his sleeve. We got a very strong eight minutes out of this simple case of mistaken identity.

6. **Reversed Roles** A reversed role sketch would have Robin Hood as the villain and the Sheriff of Nottingham as the good guy. Or one where a female office boss tries to get a young male employee drunk so she can seduce him. Or where a new servant is taken on who is so masterful that he (or she) actually governs the household and treats the employers as servants. Or, along the same lines, an ex-army officer working for a boss that was formerly his orderly and who is enjoying his revenge. A situation

depicted in that old Bing Crosby song *I've got the guy who used to be my Captain, working for me now.*

7. **True Thoughts** This form of sketch picks someone like a civil servant and gives an example of his typical dialogue and then shows what he really means. It can be done, for instance, about car salesmen:

What He Says: This car will go as fast as 200 mph.
What He Means: If pushed off the top of a skyscraper.

What He Says: This car would stop on a penny.
What He Means: It hasn't the power to get over it.

What He Says: It's air conditioned.
What He Means: There's a lot of holes in the bodywork.

A further example would be the travel agent:

What He Says: On the cruise you'll eat at the Captain's table.
What He Means: It's the only table there is.

What He Says: You'll hear a language you've never heard before.
What He Means: If you forget to tip the waiters or cab drivers.

What He Says: You'll watch the natives diving for money.
What He Means: Straight into your wallet.

8. **Collection of Cameos** A good example of this would be a collection of little cameos or quickies about how different nationals might react to an impending air crash. It could be made topical by having the reason for engine failure as suddenly running out of petrol.

9. **Transposition** The trick behind this kind of sketch is to choose a type of trade or profession or personality that has definitely accepted traits, then to transpose them into some other place where those traits would be incongruous.

For instance, if we took a tough army training sergeant and made him head waiter at a fashionable restaurant we could have some fun with the idea. Similarly we could wring laughs out of making a bus driver or conductor a steward in an aeroplane in flight. 'There's too many of you in here. Some of you will have to get off!'

10. **Character** This is the sketch where one uses a definite funny character and puts them in a normal situation. Red Skelton and Sid Caesar used to specialise in this. Very often writers use camp homosexual type characters in situations that might normally require tough men. Camp characters are always certain to get a laugh. But new writers tend to use them too often.

11. **Out of Character** Comedians like Johnny Carson, Bob Hope, Jack Benny or Jimmy Durante never did lose their own individual characters when playing parts in sketches. They often got more laughs out of the supposed ad libs than the gags written for the sketch itself. You'll be surprised to learn that most of those ad libs were actually written in by the script-writer. They are cleverly placed to *seem* like ad libs. The out-of-character lines that seem to be ad libbed are the real mainstay of the sketch. They get the biggest laughs. And they were either put in by the writer in the first instance, or added in during rehearsals. It's a tribute to the acting ability of these stars that they can make them seem as though they were thought up on the spot.

12. **Visual** Visual comedy will be dealt with extensively in the chapter on writing for foreign markets.

13. **Period** Sketches that feature, say, the Count of Monte Cristo, Casanova, Al Capone or Henry VIII do not need to have a gimmick. They just need funny scripts. The thing that distinguishes them from each other is the way the comedian plays them. And it's the writer's job to script them in the style of that particular comedian. I did one in which two guest male stars on a show said they were both promised the role of Henry VIII in the final sketch. So, in order to appease them, the host of the show made them both Henry IV's with just three wives each. The trick worked well.

14. **Underplay** This kind of sketch usually depicts the stoical English type whom nothing can upset. Come what may, he always manages to maintain his equilibrium. I wrote a series of sketches built round an aging Colonel and his even older butler. One of the sketches had them in an army bunker under heavy

shelling and bombing. The Colonel was more concerned about his meal being right than the war going on outside. He kept sending the butler out through the muck, mire and bomb blasts to get different condiments, cutlery and other trivial things needed to make his meal exactly right. Each time the butler returned with his clothes more tattered and more bandages and splints on him, but never made any reference to them. His only concern was getting the meal right for his master. It ended with his hobbling in on crutches and apologising for being so long getting the sugar for the coffee. 'I'm afraid you'll have to get the brandy yourself, sir.' 'Get it myself, Smethers? Why on earth should I?' 'Because sir . . . I've been shot,' and the butler collapsed on the spot.

15. **Nervous** The nervous sketch is one in which the comedian is thrown into a panic trying to stop something happening. One I wrote for comic Leslie Crowther (the English Dick Van Dyke) epitomises this fairly well. Leslie was expecting a visit from his uncle who loved to play practical jokes. This time Leslie planned to get his own back and booby trapped the place. The phone would spout water . . . the door handle would give off an electric shock . . . the chair by the phone would collapse under the uncle's weight . . . the towel in the bathroom would have soot all over it . . . and the door to the toilet had a bucket of flour perched over it. Then a policeman turned up because someone had reported seeing a prowler around the house. He insisted on searching the place. The comedy came from Leslie's panic in trying to avoid the booby traps happening to the policeman. The only way he could do this was by getting them to happen to himself. And when he was covered in flour, soot and water he then discovered that the policeman was really just an actor sent by the uncle as yet another practical joke.

Those fifteen forms of sketches will give you an idea of just how wide open the field is. Almost any subject can be used for the basis of a sketch. But you will have observed that none of the examples I gave you called for more than one basic set and I also kept to a minimum of characters. The producers of those sketches had no budget problems. Nor did they have to worry about whether the weather outside made the light good enough for filming. These considerations on your part can make that vital difference between a sale and a rejection.

When you set out to write a sketch the first thing you must decide on is a subject. You'll probably soon realise that whatever subject you pick will have been covered by other writers before you. So you'll have to think of a different approach. For instance, many writers have done sketches about driving lessons, baby sitters or Robin Hood and Little John. But to my knowledge there's never been one with a woman teaching a man to drive the way women drivers traditionally do . . . or a baby sitter finding that his/her charge for the evening is a baby gorilla instead of a child. And I don't recall anyone having Robin Hood and Little John talk and act like TV Detectives Lieutenant Columbo and Marshall McLoud while trying to find where the Sheriff has hidden the kidnapped Maid Marian.

And what about a send-up of any detective series with the characters using as much gadgetry as they did on *The Man from U.N.C.L.E.*? You'd have everyone communicating with each other by talking through their fountain pens or the heels of their shoes or their tie clips. It could possibly end with the phone ringing and none of them recognising what it is.

Someone once said that you start out writing a sketch by asking yourself, 'What would happen if . . .?' For example, what would happen if the props in a TV murder mystery got mixed up because they had a new Stage Manager on the show? The gun might be in the desk drawer where the all-important diary should be. And the diary would be in the murderer's pocket where the gun should be. The key doesn't fit the door and the night-intruder has to climb through the glassless window. There's just a vase of flowers where the phone should be. Sounds crazy? Of course it does. But it's the basis of one of the funniest sketches that Dick Vosburgh and I ever wrote together. We did the murder scene straight first for a minute and then showed what would happen if there was a new Stage Manager who wasn't as competent as he should be.

The actors bluffed it through, holding the diary like a gun: 'I warn you, Carson, this thing's loaded!' And reading from the gun as though it was a diary. Talking into the vase of flowers as though it was a phone. Those, and the careless switching over of several other important props, made for a hilarious six minutes.

What would happen if an actor and actress had to do a passionate love scene and one of them had a shocking cold which the other one didn't want to catch? The words of love to one another would be passionate, but they would be contrary to the actions.

What would happen if, in a stage play, the curtain got stuck and was only up as high as the knees of the performers? They'd carry on saying their lines and acting normally, but all we'd see is their legs. It's funny and intriguing if an actress in the scene

61

says, 'George, tonight I'm going to show you something you've never seen before. There! What do you think of them?' And the actor says, 'By golly, they really are beauties. And so big, too!' You'd get big laughs before he continues with, 'I've never seen such big earrings.' There's all sorts of permutations on the dialogue that could make this kind of sketch exceedingly funny.

We know that if two men crash their cars into each other there may well be a fight as to whose fault it was. But supposing it was two ladies. Would they perhaps start out angry and then one say, 'Ooh, I like your hair. Where do you have it done?' 'At Henri's in the High Street. Just next to that new fashion boutique. My, that's a beautiful coat you've got on. I bet you got that in Bond Street.' 'No, as a matter of fact I've found a darling little tailor in Finchley. Makes the most fabulous clothes — and he's so reasonable.' 'You must give me his address. And in return, I'll give you a tip. They're selling tinned peaches at threepence off at Tesco.' You can imagine the scene. Their two cars blocking the road and holding up other traffic while the ladies discuss each other's hair, clothes and shopping.

I sold a sketch to several countries in which the comedienne played a nurse who is helping out in the operating theatre for the first time and suddenly discovers that the patient is her favourite pop star. She's so excited that she does everything wrong and almost kills the poor fellow. Then she goes right off him because, in his semi-conscious state, he doesn't respond to her request for his autograph.

Another sketch starring a comedienne had her playing the part of the shorthand recorder in a law court who fancies the man in the dock and refuses to write down anything bad said against him. Everytime she has to read back what's been said, she has included her own comments and added her own adjectives to describe the person who spoke: 'the evil-looking prosecuting counsel'; 'the handsome, blue-eyed, obviously innocent defendant'; 'his over-painted, brassy-looking wife'. She heckles the witnesses for the prosecution and cheers anything said in favour of the accused.

Still in the courtroom, I wrote a sketch about the judge in a case involving a very sexy lady defendant. From the moment she crosses her legs and heaves her bosom in his direction, he falls madly in love with her and belittles all evidence against her while over-exaggerating the importance of the tiny amount of evidence in her favour. It had a fair amount of visual comedy in it with the Judge having to fan himself with his wig every time she heaved her bosom, and his hiding or deliberately misinterpreting, and even destroying, any really convincing item of exhibit evidence in favour of the prosecutor's case.

Here are some sketch ideas suggested by my former students.

We have such things as tree surgeons, and people now do talk to their plants. So why not a sketch about a plant psychiatrist? People bringing in their ailing flowers and pot plants for psychiatric treatment.

Now that there are eight different fare structures on airline flights you often find that the fellow sitting next to you has paid as little as half what you've paid for the very same journey. But what you paid entitles you to some extra perks. The sketch suggested was from the viewpoint of the poor harrassed air hostess trying to figure out who is entitled to what extra services for the different fares they've paid.

Many people spend their annual holiday at a health farm where they go to suffer the agonies of being underfed and over-exercised to slim off the odd pound or two. The suggestion was a health farm that does the reverse. A place where slim people go to gain weight and feel complimented when anyone told them they were getting fat.

We have TV licence detector vans which travel round spying on whether people are using television sets without having a current licence. How about a marriage licence detector van? It would be spying on bedrooms and challenging their occupants to prove they were married.

Think up your own ideas like those I've just given you. Make your list of every single thing you can think of that is related to the subject. Go through the list over and over again till you have enough funny thoughts down on paper.

The next thing to do is work out a logical order for them. Then all you need is a good strong ending. There are no set methods for getting good endings. If there were, most of us would too easily guess the end of every sketch we ever see on TV. We can't because good endings have the element of surprise. As in gag writing, you should be able to lead your audience up the garden path. Set their minds in one direction and then suddenly switch to another direction entirely. I've just seen a sketch that serves as a good example. It had a French girl returning to comedian Ronnie Corbett after a quarrel. She begs him to forgive her and take her back. He agrees. Now, up to this point we have been led by the writer to believe they are husband and wife or at least lovers. But then the writer surprises us by having Ronnie go to the door and shout, 'Darling, the maid's back!'

Sometimes writers resort to using a standard form of tag in which the situation restarts at the end. You've seen this done many times. A salesman, for instance, cries about not making a sale and his fear of losing his job in order to coerce a customer into buying something. The customer buys, the salesman thanks him profusely for saving his livelihood. Then that customer leaves the shop and the salesman ends the sketch by using the same speil on the next one.

Another familiar form is the running gag which is planted earlier in the show. I used this where an actor had sung badly. We did a few insult gags about how bad a singer he was. Then, in the final sketch, a character refused to talk under severe interrogation. He doesn't succumb to normal forms of torture, but finally gives in under the threat of the worst torture imaginable . . . we show that torture to be the actor singing again.

These are some of the tricks and devices you can use to get out of trouble. But they shouldn't be necessary if you can think of a good natural tag. Once you've decided on what to write there comes the moment of truth when you have actually got to put pen to paper.

What I do at that stage is spend several hours typing out every possible facet I can think of connected with that person in that situation. Many I know will not work or are too childish or too subtle, but I put them down anyway to eliminate them. By the time I've filled about three pages I'll break off for a cup of tea and then return to my desk and read it all through. That's when I tick off the parts that may fit. I say 'may' because there are some extremely funny thoughts that just don't fit in. Probably because they'd take so long to set up that you just haven't got room for them in a four or five minute sketch.

I then type out the ticked off items and use them as my nucleus to build up another three pages. It's the same process again. Ticking off. Eliminating and developing and expanding the ideas, gags and bits of business that I've settled on. Now the sketch starts to take shape and I try and type it through from beginning to end. Then I hone it, cutting out the dead wood and try to keep it down to the time I want it. It's funny, but most writers will agree that it's far easier to write a long sketch than it is a short one. So I keep all the bits I cut out in a file to replace any parts that the comedian or producer might not like at the first read-through. That's how it's done. Try it and you should find that it'll all fit together like a jigsaw puzzle. The elements for a good sketch are there in your mind, you just have to put them on paper and jiggle them around to get them in the right order.

I hope I have furnished you with enough ideas to inspire your own. With luck, you'll be itching to grab a pencil and pad and start work on a series of black-outs, quickies or even a sketch.

Here is a sample of what a finished sketch looks like. It's one done by Les Dawson on television. The sex roles are reversed with the female being the hunter.

The Set: A Plush Executive Office.

Helen Sturdley, a thirty-five-year-old business lady, is behind her plush desk talking to her husband on the phone.

Helen: (To phone) I'm awfully sorry about this, darling, but I'm having to work late again tonight. Kiss the children goodnight for me . . . and don't wait up, I might be late. Goodbye, darling.

She puts the phone down with a self-satisfied smile. Preens her hair and looks at her make-up mirror to be sure she looks right. Then she buzzes the intercom on her desk.

We hear Les's shy voice over the intercom.

Les: (Voice only) Yes, Mrs Sturdley?
Helen: (To intercom) Come in here, will you, Cyril.
Les: (Voice only) It's six o'clock. I was just going home.
Helen: Ah, well, I want you to stay a bit late tonight. I've some things for you to do. Come in, will you.

A couple of seconds later Les enters. He has his hair parted in the middle. He wears thick lensed spectacles and generally looks a shy type. He carries a notepad and pencil in his hand.

Les: I've brought my notepad and pencil.
Helen: (Leers at him lecherously) Good. Sit down, my dear.

Les sits on a chair on the opposite side of the desk.

Helen pats the seat of a chair next to her meaning him to sit on it.

Helen: Over here, Cyril. Then I can talk softly.
Les: (Moving to other chair) Oh, is it confidential?
Helen: Very.

Les sits in the chair with his notepad and pencil poised.

Les: I'm ready.
Helen: Good. So am I! Tell me, do you always wear those glasses?
Les: Not always.
Helen: Take them off.
Les: (Surprised) What?
Helen: Take them off. Surely you've been asked to take them off before.
Les: (Takes off glasses shyly) I . . . I don't usually work with my eyes naked. But I'll do the best I can. *(Poised again with notepad and pencil)* Shall we get started?
Helen: All in good time. *(Seductively)* You know, you're much more handsome without those glasses.

She puts her hand on his knee. Les is shocked and removes her hand at once.

Les: Mrs Sturdley! I'm not that kind of a boy!
Helen: You want promotion, don't you?
Les: I'd like to think I was getting it on my merits.
Helen: Oh, you *will*, I assure you.

She takes two prepared glasses of whisky from

her desk drawer. She gives Les the one that is full, her own is only half filled.

Helen: Have a little whisky with me.
Les: (Declining the offer) No thank you. I never drink when I'm working.
Helen: Regard this as your coffee break.

Les gets up from the chair.

Helen: Where are you going?
Les: To make a cup of coffee.

She pulls him back into the chair.

Helen: Coffee break's over!

Helen just stares at him lecherously for a few seconds and then rubs her hand on his face. He leans back in his chair trying to back away from her hand.

Les: Mrs Sturdley, if you're going to give me dictation, please do it now. I promised my mother I'd be home early tonight. It's my turn to go to the laundrette.

She totally ignores what he said.

Helen: You know, Cyril, you're much too intelligent to be wasted on a job like this. A man with your determination and ability should be sitting right here in the managing director's chair.
Les: That's . . . that's very flattering of you.
Helen: No, I mean it. Go on, try it for size.

She gets up and gestures for him to sit in her chair.

Les: All right, if you like.

He sits in her chair and she immediately sits down on his lap.

Helen: There. Isn't that much better?

Les is very embarrassed.

Les: Please, Mrs Sturdley, I've got to get up now.
Helen: No, you haven't.
Les: Yes, I have.
Helen: Why have you?
Les: I'm sitting on my pencil!

She gets up to let him retrieve his pencil. He uses the opportunity to try to escape.

Les: I've just remembered, the laundrette closes at seven tonight.

She pulls him back so that this time he is sitting on her lap.

Helen: Never mind about the laundrette! *(She puts her face up against his face)* Don't you think I'm attractive?
Les: Yes, I suppose you are. I . . . I can't see very well without my glasses.

He makes a vain struggle to reach for his glasses, but she holds him back.

Helen: You could try the touch system.

She places his arm around her waist. He is getting hot and more embarrassed. He gulps.

Les: Do you mind if I loosen my tie a little?
Helen: (Undoing his tie for him) Take it off. It's a start.

She pulls his tie off and throws it away with gay abandon. Then she slowly bears down on him to kiss him. But just before the actual point of contact, the phone rings.

F/X. Phone ringing.

Helen stays in position, but reaches her arm back behind her and lifts the phone off the receiver.

Helen: (Casually to phone) Yes?

She listens for a second or two and then reacts shocked.

Helen: (To phone) What? Here? Now? Thank you.

She slams the phone down and pulls Les out of the chair.

Helen: (In a panic) My husband's downstairs on his way up here. He's violently jealous. If he catches you, he'll kill you! Quick, hide in the cupboard!

She quickly pushes Les into the cupboard He tries to protest his innocence and come out again. But she pushes him back in . . . throws his tie in after him and closes the cupboard door just in time.

Her husband enters the room suspicious and angry.

Husband: (Angry) You've tried to fool me for the last time, Helen! I've had you watched by a private detective. You've got a man in that cupboard, haven't you.
Helen: (Spreading herself in front of the cupboard door to shield it) No, of course I haven't. I don't know what you're talking about.
Husband: Don't lie to me, Helen!

He pulls her away from the cupboard door and takes a gun out of his pocket and points it at the cupboard.

Husband: Come out of that cupboard! Come out or I'll shoot! *(A two second pause)* I'll give you to a count of three. *(Counts slowly)* One . . . two . . . three . . .

*He is about to shoot as Les comes out with his
hands up . . . and is followed in quick succession
by eight other men.*

*Husband, in a state of shock continues the count
as they emerge from the cupboard.*

*Husband: (Continued) . . . four . . . five . . . six . . .
seven . . .*

*Close sketch on Les's expression of surprise as he
watches the other lovers come out behind him.*

4 / Satire

Somewhere in my bottom drawer I still have my copy of the
award we won as a team for writing *That Was The Week That
Was*. Satire became popular because it credited audiences with
intelligence. It left something to their imagination and they
enjoyed having to think for themselves. But the ratings proved
that *That Was The Week That Was* did not gain equal
popularity all over the country. The show's appeal was mainly
to an intellectual audience. The kind that likes to debunk the
establishment and see pompous dignitaries being poked fun at.

Prior to David Frost this form of comedy was usually censored
out of TV scripts as being too politically biased or in danger
of a libel suit. The only place one could see satire in those days
was in stage revue shows. Perhaps the most famous of them
was *Beyond The Fringe,* which brought to light the writing and
performing talents of Peter Cook, Dudley Moore, Jonathan
Miller and Alan Bennett.

Though it may seem rather innocuous now, that show was very controversial for its time. It might be useful for you to buy a copy of the complete *Beyond The Fringe* script which is available quite cheaply from Samuel French Ltd, the theatrical book publishers with shops in London and New York. It will give you an idea of how much more bite satire has acquired since then.

I used to describe satire as an insult with an Oxford accent. But as I got more involved with it I came to realise that it need not be insulting at all. It is at its best when just poking simple harmless fun. When Mike Yarwood did his shoulder shaking impression of Edward Heath or David Frye did his shoulder haunching impression of Richard Nixon, that was satire. There was nothing malicious in it. All they'd done was isolate familiar traits and exaggerate them.

You may remember the famous sketch about the late Ed Murrow, the TV interviewer and commentator who chain smoked throughout all his shows. The sketch was just an ordinary interview with Murrow and a guest, but with every puff at the cigarette the room got more and more clouded with smoke. It ended up so foggy that you could still hear the voices, but see nothing through the smoke.

Malcolm Muggeridge was a popular figure on British TV at that time and he had three peculiar traits which were fodder for the satirists. While talking, Muggeridge would unconsciously stroke his hair, stick his right finger in his ear occasionally and continually crack his knuckles. Mike Yarwood's impression had handfuls of hair coming out every time he stroked his head . . . his right index finger getting stained with wax or jammed in his ear . . . and the knuckle-cracking getting increasingly louder till it completely drowned out what he was saying.

This kind of fun can be made of a single person (as just shown) or a group of people. A very funny sketch on *Not the Nine O'Clock News* had a meeting of Workaholics on the same lines as Alcoholics Anonymous. One guy bemoaning the fact that his wife left him because she couldn't take any longer his coming home every night smelling of money. Another guy with telephones inside his jacket kept making and receiving business calls throughout the meeting. A third guy, a hairdresser, kept combing the other people's hair as he talked about his problem of being a compulsive worker.

You could take an important group of people like the United Nations Security Council and have fun by making them debate the unimportant decision of whether to have tea or coffee during the morning recess. With the East and West on opposing sides. Russia and America both threatening to use their vetoes if the decision goes against their own preference.

How about a court convened under the Sex Discrimination Act in which a man complains because they wouldn't accept him as a candidate for the Miss World contest?

Or complaining because most hurricanes are named after women and hardly any after men? Or even that ladies and gents toilets are a form of sex discrimination?

Peter Jones satirised tennis match commentators (not one in particular, but all of them) when he portrayed a BBC announcer who said, 'And now we take you to Wimbledon for a commentary on the Centre Court match . . .' There was an embarrassing pause and Peter said, 'Ah, there appears to be a technical hitch and while we're trying to fix it they've asked me to fill in for a moment or two. Now what can I tell you . . .?' Then he went on to describe the studio he was in, the furniture in it, the temperature . . . and then finally the progress of two flies chasing each other across the ceiling. All done using the tones, inflections, spasmodic excitement and vernacular language of a tennis commentary. It was both clever and funny.

Bob Newhardt's TV series used sketches which depended largely on satire for their humour. The comedy pinpointed the foibles of certain groups. He'd have a sketch where postal sorters were taught to manhandle all fragile parcels so that the contents would break. Another sketch had taxi drivers being taught to take the longest possible route and being rehearsed in hard-luck stories to evoke sympathy from the passenger and get a bigger tip. He'd have a group of lawyers being taught to write letters in anything but plain English so that you'd be forced to hire another lawyer to decipher what they were saying.

Newhardt would have a doctor calling in another for a second opinion if you just asked him the time. Or a policeman warning you of your rights before answering your enquiry for street directions.

To find fuel for your own satire you should make out a list of popular or generally accepted beliefs and then stretch them to the point of incongruity. For instance, it's thought that the Japanese are leading the world in electronics and motor cars. They can produce them cheaper than most other nations. Suppose they went into the portable home business too. Can you imagine the Queen of England living in a Japanese-style Buckingham Palace? Or the American President in a Japanese-style White House? The Queen would have a cushion on the floor instead of a throne. She would knight people with a sabre

73

instead of a sword. The Changing of the Guard would be Samurai instead of Coldstream Guards with bamboo sentry boxes.

Or you might marry some current news items together. There's a recent announcement that scientists are very close to being able to tell a baby's sex before it is actually born. We also hear that the number of gays coming out of the closet is growing every year. The obvious thought there is that while it's getting easier to tell a human's sex before they're born, it's getting harder when they're about twenty years old.

Someone in the government suggested that instead of sending so many offenders to our overcrowded prisons, they ought to be made to do some sort of community work instead. Like what? Well, there's a big shortage of policemen. Could we make these criminals work as part time policemen? It might lend itself to some funny situations. And what about the women offenders? Could making them into prostitutes be called using them for community work?

And what about our prisons being so overcrowded that you have to book your place before you commit your crime? Can you imagine a sketch in which a potential criminal hops into his local police station and has a discussion with the desk sergeant about how serious a crime he'll have to commit to get into one of the more popular prisons. And when is the best time to commit it. And possibly even suggesting bribing the sergeant to be sure of a place.

It's important that the subject you pick be well enough known to your audience. If you said, 'The Beatles split up was because of a row over their manager. One of them thought there was a worm in the Apple.' That only registers with the audience if they know that the Beatles' jointly held company was called Apple.

Similarly, if you had Marlon Brando doing a commercial for butter it would only be funny if the people watching knew of the erotic scene Brando took part in in the film *Last Tango in Paris*.

Television commercials are a great target for satire. Benny Hill has probably made more money out of guying commercials than the owners of the products ever did. A sketch I particularly remember from *Beyond the Fringe* had the four stars of that revue dressed up as tough mariners doing a very butch commercial for a certain tobacco and, as soon as they knew the cameras were off them, they reverted to their natural limp-wristed camp characters.

A brand of margarine once advertised that every time you

buy a packet of their product they would give three pennies to the Wildlife Fund. It may be a sick thought, but what immediately springs to mind is that some cigarette manufacturer might follow it by offering, 'For every packet of our cigarettes you buy we'll donate a penny to Cancer Research.'

You've probably seen the quickies done on *Laugh-In* where two delegates have a bloody battle to decide who should sit where at a Peace Conference. Or a room full of people paying a hundred dollars each for a ten course meal to support the starving nations. The humour in these examples comes from the irony of the situation.

A good source for spotting subjects for satire is the readers' letters columns in the daily papers. There's always someone pointing out the unexpected side of a current news item. I would also recommend a subscription to *Private Eye, Mad Magazine* and *National Lampoon*, which all specialise in satirical articles.

A favourite form of satire often used on TV shows is to dig back through the film archives and find a speech by a politician who has recently risen in the ranks. You show the promises or pledges they made several years ago before they took office and compare it to their actions now. It's usually hilarious and often quite cruel. Especially as these film clips are sometimes taken completely out of context and appear to mean the complete opposite to what they actually intended.

That Was The Week That Was used this gimmick frequently and it reached the point where the public switched the show on like that maniacal woman knitting while watching the French Revolution. They thirsted for blood and wouldn't be satisfied unless one public figure was slaughtered each week.

Used this way, satire can be a dangerous weapon. A cowardly one, too, because the victim's not there to defend himself. But as *Private Eye* has found out many times to its cost, some victims have expert lawyers who will drag you into court if you go just that little bit too far.

Another idea for a satirical sketch could be two wrestlers stopping in the middle of a brutal match because one complains that the other man isn't sticking to script. 'It was *my* turn to get *you* in the half Nelson.' And their argument leads into them wrestling for real.

Or how about a send-up of the BBC intellectual TV quiz show *Mastermind*? The four contestants would all be government ministers being questioned on the subject of their own particular department. They'd all give either evasive or ambiguous answers.

You could do a take-off of *This Is Your Life* with militant union leader Arthur Scargill as the subject for the show. You'd trace his life through from his nursery days when he brought the other babies out on strike. At school he'd have had the other kids picketing outside the classrooms for shorter homework. Every stage of his life would show him bringing people out on strike. The programme would end with the M.C., Eamonn Andrews (Ralph Edwards in America), talking to an empty studio because Scargill had brought the camera crew and audience out on strike too.

Here's a short satirical sketch written for the original *Three Of A Kind* series starring Mike Yarwood, Lulu and Ray Fell. Ray Fell and Lulu played Harry and Gladys, two union shop stewards who had been courting for some time.

The Set.   Section of a Factory Canteen.   Day.

Gladys and Harry are seated at a table sipping their cups of tea. She is dressed in overalls and he in a boiler suit.

Gladys: Tea's off colour again today.
Harry: No, it isn't. It's always been this shade of grey. Mind you, the shop steward of the cutting room complained to the management about it yesterday.
Gladys: And did they change anything?
Harry: Yeah. The shop steward of the cutting room. I don't know, us shop stewards don't seem to have the pull we used to in this place.
Gladys: That's true enough. Every time I go to the guv'nor and ask for something, I always get the same answer.
Harry: What's that?
Gladys: He says he'll say yes if I do.
Harry: All them guv'nors are the same — ruddy liberty takers.
Glaldys: Yeah. I don't mind this 'labour and management walking hand in hand' bit. But he always wants to go much further.
Harry: Exploitation of the workers — that's what it is. Next time you go by him and he puts his hand out — you tell me.

76

Gladys: Why? What'll you do?

Harry: Make his teeth come out in sympathy.

Gladys: Thanks, Harry. Say, Harry, how long have we known each other?

Harry: Let's see now. We met about fifteen months ago on that pay-claim walk-out.

Gladys: That's right.

Harry: And we've been walking out together ever since.

Gladys: Remember when we both became shop stewards — how we used to have them secret meetings?

Harry: Down on the factory floor. Then later we used to get together round your place of an evening.

Gladys: My Mum liked you right from the beginning. She used to blow her whistle and pull the whole family out — so we could snog alone in the living room.

Harry: But your Dad was a bit of a stickler, wasn't he? I mean, I've never known another girl whose old man made me clock in and out every evening.

Gladys: Yeah, but he did let you have time and a half on Sundays. Do you remember what he said when you asked him for extra snogging time?

Harry: He said I couldn't have any. I'd just have to do more in the time I'd got.

Gladys: (Change of tone) Well, Harry, after fifteen months of courtship, you haven't yet said anything serious to me.

Harry: What about it?

Gladys: Exactly. That's all you ever say. Well, last night my parents and I took a secret vote. And we've come out in favour of a change in my relationship with you.

Harry: What sort of change, Glad?

Gladys: Well, for the time being, a period of severe restraint.

Harry: Oh no, Glad. Not snogging to rule!

Gladys: Yes, Harry. And if there's no results at the end of that — the ultimate weapon.

Harry: The freeze?

Gladys: The freeze. A complete withdrawal of personnel.

Harry: Deliberate absenteeism. Without so much as a golden handshake. This is a case of blatant victimisation.

Gladys: Well, I'm all for following a policy of progress, Harry. I want to get married and go into production of my own. Can't you understand Harry? I'm fed up being your brother — I want to be your wife!

Harry: You mean you want to tie me down to one woman? No longer Harry Perkins — one for all. You want me — all for one.

Gladys: That's right.

Harry: I've got to make all me other girl friends redundant?

Gladys: Those are my terms. I don't believe in work sharing.

Harry: Well, all right then, Glad. I can understand your desire for security — and I shall not shirk my responsibilities. *(Clears throat)* Gladys Dingwall — will you share a union card with me?

Gladys: (Excited) Oh Harry, do you mean it?

Harry: Yes — this is an official proposal. Perhaps you would be good enough to refer it back to your committee at home — and let me have their decision in due course.

Gladys: Delighted as I am — I still think we should adhere to traditional procedure.

Harry: All right — I'll form a delegation of one and nip round to your Dad during the lunch hour.

Gladys: Dad's a reasonable man — I'm sure he'll offer you an amicable settlement. As long as you're true to me.

Harry: Gladys, I'm a man of my word. I fully agree to abide by the rules and bye-laws as laid down in the marriage certificate. And furthermore, I shall strictly regard the agreement relating to demarcation of duties.

Gladys: What agreement's that, Harry?

Harry: That I go to work and you have the babies.

Gladys: Right, Harry. Don't you think this calls for a little celebration?

Harry: Yes. *(Shouts)* A free mug of tea for everybody — we're celebrating. The shop steward of the machine shop . . .

> *Gladys: (Shouts)* And the shop stewardess of the clerical section . . .
> *Harry & Gladys: (Together)* Are amalgamating!

They bang their mugs together and drink.

Play Off Music.

That sketch was easy to write with the help of a list of all the union phraseology reported in newspaper stories at the time, and then fitting them in as part of the expected conversation of a courting couple.

Try listing the vernacular phrases of any trade or profession and fitting it into a different situation. It's a simple and effective way to get laughs.

5 / Visual Comedy for Foreign Markets

By far the most popular of all comedy is the visual kind. Sometimes called comedy 'business'. It's the only form that can be fully appreciated by knave and king alike. And it has no language barriers. That's why Charlie Chaplin, Laurel and Hardy, Buster Keaton became such great international stars.

In music there is an internationally agreed code with crotchets, minims, quavers, sharps, flats and so on, by which a composer can get his work understood by everyone. Written music is itself an international language. There is even a language for choreographers in which they record their dance routines. And, in recent years, road signs have been designed so all foreigners can understand them. But though English is supposed to be the 'International Language' as far as politics and commerce is concerned, you'll find it doesn't work that easily selling comedy.

Before actually getting on to visual comedy, let's dwell for a moment or two with the language problems you could encounter. In Chapter One we considered gags on the theme of automobiles. But compare our British terms to those used by the Americans (who are supposed to speak English), and you'll see how some of our gags wouldn't be understood by them and vice versa. What we call a bonnet they call a hood. Our boot is their trunk . . . . petrol is gasoline . . . gear levers are gear shifts. We put it into gear . . . they throw it into gear. We turn left or right . . . they make a left or right. They spell tyres as tires. What we call motorways they call highways, freeways or turnpikes. Most of their highways have toll charges, virtually unknown in Britain. We're also unfamiliar with the stealing of hubcaps which is the favourite pastime of American juvenile delinquents. They don't use L plates so there's no way of knowing if the chap in front of you is a learner driver. Their number plates are called licence plates and are renewed annually for about two hundred dollars as the equivalent of our road fund licence. And there are many more differences. So obviously some British gags about driving wouldn't be understood in America and some of Bob Hope's gags about American cars and their drivers go way over our heads.

On my first visit to New York way back in 1956 I really epitomised the innocent abroad. I got gales of laughter from my female host when I asked her to 'knock me up at seven in the morning', not knowing that to knock someone up is the American expression for making them pregnant. And when offered a choice of flavoured yoghurts I said I preferred cherries. More laughter. They call virgins, cherries. I also learned that prostitutes are called hookers or barflies, that if a girl is referred to as being 'out of sight' then one ought to get a look at her because she's really worth looking at. And that if she's 'something else' that also means she's good looking. The term 'homely' when used to describe a girl is most ungallant and means she's definitely plain, or, to use another Americanism, 'she's a dog'. When the Americans talk of crumpet they mean those muffin things you eat with tea, and not a girl of easy virtue, which they call 'a piece of tail'.

So if you're aiming to write for foreign markets it would be just as well to do some research or your gags might fall flat or get laughs in the wrong places. If you're in any doubt, the information service at any foreign embassy won't charge you a thing to answer your queries.

When I am writing the first time for a foreign country, I either phone or write to their embassy asking them whether my script will be fully understandable in their country. They've been most helpful in setting me right when I've put down a word or phrase that has, in their language, an ambiguous meaning. Of if they have no equivalent word or phrase that it can be translated to. Here's a gag I used on TV for both British comedians Tommy Cooper and Dick Emery which wasn't workable on the Continent. I had Tommy drive on in a tiny Messerschmidt bubble car and do a whole comedy routine about the great gadgets that were built into it.

He spoke about the phone at the back, and at that moment it rang. He lifted the receiver, listened to the voice at the other end and then rested the phone down while he went round to look at the number plates. Then he picked up the phone again and said, 'Sorry, you've got the wrong number.' This didn't work because just about everywhere in Europe they say, 'Sorry, you have been mis-connected' not, 'Sorry, wrong number.' And unless the word 'number' is in the tag line the gag fails.

There are hundreds of idiomatic phrases in common usage in the English language today. Some must be completely incomprehensible to foreigners. Why, for instance, when someone tells us something we don't believe do we say, 'In a pig's eye!' I've never known why we refer to people who bore us as being a 'pain in the neck'. Or why, if we're going to the local pub we say, 'I'm just *slipping* out for a quick one.' If you take these phrases literally they don't make sense. No doubt at school you were told the howler of the Frenchman who was looking out of the window of an English train when another train started speeding towards them on the next track. A fellow passenger shouted 'Look out!' So he looked further out and got his head chopped off.

Now that we've established that puns and word plays don't sell to Europe, you'll want to know what does sell. Funny ideas sell. I mean routines, sketches, and whole shows that are based on comic ideas and don't rely on gags put in along the way. That must be your rule when writing for foreign markets. Your sketches must have a funny basis so that the comedian's action or reaction is universally funny. Here are 10 sketches that were used on TV in Europe recently.

1. **The Nervous Waiter** An old waiter keeps bringing the customer the wrong things, but is so terrified of the cook that he pleads with the customer to accept the wrong dishes rather than have him lose his job. The customer gets tomato omelette though he hates tomatoes — with chips though he's on a diet. And his dessert contains strawberries which he is allergic to. He reluctantly

agrees to eat all these things to save the waiter's job for him. (Originally done with Dick Emery playing his Lampwick character as the waiter.)

2. **The Little Brother** A man has invited his new girlfriend round to his flat for what he hopes will be an evening of love-making. He bribes his kid brother to stay in his own room playing with his toys so that they won't be disturbed. But each time the man gets the girl ready, the kid brother finds another reason to come in and ruins the mood. Five times this happens and every time the kid has to be bribed more and more to go back to his room. Finally the elder brother decides that he'll get no peace (or piece) at home so he'll take the girl to the back row of the pictures instead. Then he realises that he can't afford it as all his money has gone on bribes. So the rather precocious kid brother bribes him to stay at home while he himself takes the girl to the pictures. (Originally done with Mike Winters as the elder brother and Bernie Winters in short trousers as the kid.)

3. **The Spy School** This one had the comedian being taught to be a spy at a spy training school. It involved unarmed combat, memory tests, enduring torture and trying to resist giving away vital information while being seduced by a beautiful girl. The tutor did everything perfectly well and the comic got his laughs by doing it badly in comparison. But the idea of a school that trains simple men to become James Bonds is funny in itself.

4. **The Opera Box** A rather low-brow good-natured Cockney type is given a ticket to the opera and finds himself sharing a theatre box with a very highbrow husband and wife dressed for the occasion with white tie, tails and tiara. He inadvertently continues to annoy them with his offers to share his packet of crisps and his (to them) sacrilegious remarks about the performers and banal questions about what they are singing and doing. Again the comedy came from the contrast between the very formal couple who worshipped everything about the opera and the seemingly unappreciative 'commoner' who didn't understand what it was all about.

5. **The Insurance Salesman** A shy insurance man turns up for an appointment with a prospective client and has to talk to the man in the bathroom because he got up late and is still shaving. This is in itself a funny situation. It becomes funnier when the

man finds that he has to sit down on the toilet in order to read out information and work out figures from the documents in his briefcase. His embarrassment increases even further when the client's wife comes in to have a shower and starts to divest herself of her clothes. The salesman tries to pretend she isn't there but the vital statistics get included in the figures he is adding up. She closes the shower curtains, to his relief. But very soon the embarrassment gets even more intense as she drops the soap and asks his help to feel around in the water to find it. He does this with one hand while firmly slapping the other over his eyes. At no time do the husband or wife show any signs of the situation being unusual as far as they are concerned. If they did the sketch wouldn't be funny.

6. **The Window Cleaner** This one is the reverse situation. A window cleaner is working on a block of flats and gets stuck inside a bedroom when the window gets jammed. It is the flat of an exceedingly jealous husband who is known to be violent and would never accept such a simple explanation. He has caught his wife with a lover in the bedroom before and put him in hospital. The comedy comes from the wife's attempts to help the window cleaner escape. That's impossible, so she keeps changing his hiding place to avoid him being found by the husband. It's what I call 'nervous comedy', because the laughs are at the nervousness of the wife and the window cleaner as the bully of a husband unsuspectingly almost finds him.

7. **The Butler and the Maid** This one is set at a fashionable dinner party where the very posh guests are seated round the table and are being served by the butler and the maid who are husband and wife. The butler casually glances down the front of one of the guests' low cut gown and this starts a row between them. But the comedy came from hearing the row taking place offstage in the kitchen. Their voices were raised at each other and everytime they reappeared to serve the next course the butler would have half of it poured over him by the wife. But nobody ever remarked on it and their manner, outside the kitchen, was always of the utmost politeness to each other while obviously concealing dreaded hatred.

The interesting point here is that it is often much funnier not to see something happen but merely to see the results of it. We never actually see the maid pour the dish of spaghetti over the butler but we imagine it happening. Then we laugh when we see him coming back into the dining room with spaghetti all over his hair and it's even funnier because everyone ignores it.

(Originally this sketch was done by Peter Sellers and Hattie Jacques and later by Alfred Marks and Paddie O'Neil.)

8. **The Airport Hotel** With the advent of Jumbo Jets a hotel which was built some way from the airport now finds itself just at the end of the extended runway. Everytime a plane takes off the noise is deafening and the pots and pans and crockery in the kitchen shake and fall. The manager cannot keep any kitchen staff.

The comedian arrives straight from the Employment Office unaware of the hazards of the job. He says straight away that he gave up his job in town because he couldn't stand the traffic noise. The hotel manager has to keep the comedian working there or he'll have to close the place. So the basis of the sketch is the attempts of himself and his assistant manager to explain away the noises and pretend the shaking isn't happening, in the hope they'll fool the comedian that he's imagining it. This is yet another 'nervous comedy' sketch, but here the comedian plays the opposite role to the one in the window cleaner sketch.

9. **Cell Mates** An effeminate poetry-loving convict has decorated his cell with chintz curtains, pictures on the wall, floral quilt etc. The warden puts a rough, tough convict in to share with him. The new arrival wants to escape and the effeminate one tries to persuade him to stay and join in the poetry reading, needlework and choral society classes. The strong contrast between the two men and their aims in life are what makes the comedy in this sketch.

10. **The Reunion Meal** Three ex-army buddies who have remained friends over the years have met for a drink every Christmas. This year they've decided to extend it to a meal with their wives at a fashionable restaurant. Everything goes well until the bill arrives, and each of the men offers to pay for them all. The others won't hear of it and they finally agree to just pay their own share. One wife says, 'Helen had peas and I didn't, so they have to pay more than us.' And Helen says, 'But you had cream on your trifle and I didn't so you've got more to pay for that.' Each of the wives finds reasons why her husband is entitled to pay less than the others. The wives argue. Their husbands are obliged to stand by their wives in the arguments and what set out to be a happy celebration meal, develops into a virtual war just because they brought their wives with them.

I think that's a fair cross section of sketches built on funny ideas that would translate into any language without losing anything. One of the best ways of finding out whether a sketch might sell to the Continent is to do a brief synopsis of it, as I've just done. Then ask yourself whether the *premise* of it is funny. Next ask yourself whether the *subject* is universally known. For instance, a hilarious sketch about golf wouldn't mean a thing in Holland where the game is hardly known. A sketch that sends up Robin Hood, the Scarlet Pimpernel, William Tell or Sherlock Holmes might sell, whereas one sending up Pickwick, Rob Roy, Guy Fawkes or Dorian Gray definitely wouldn't. The Continentals don't know about them. If in doubt about a subject ask the embassy, or a national of the country, if you know one.

* * *

Now let's delve a little into how a writer creates visual pictures. Over and over again I've used the word 'contrast' as the basis for most television comedy. It's a fact that we tend to laugh at things because they are different from what we expected them to be. If Queen Elizabeth and Prince Philip were to visit a naval establishment, she would wear a fashionable gown and he would wear his admiral's uniform. But if she wore the uniform and he wore the gown, it would look funny. The *Monty Python's Flying Circus* series used this kind of thing a lot for laughs.

If a ship were dressed overall with flags it would look decorative but not funny. But if, instead of flags on the line there was the family washing (Long Johns, bras, pants and socks) hanging out to dry, it would look funny. Again it differs from what we expect and are used to.

Supposing a man who is five foot six and of medium build walks down a street, no-one would even notice him. He is definitely not funny. But if he were suddenly joined by his wife who is six foot three and weighs twenty stone, he becomes funny by contrast.

Let us imagine two middle-aged men gossiping to each other across a window sill. One is inside the house leaning with his elbow on the sill and the other man is on the outside with his elbow on the sill looking in. This is quite normal. You wouldn't laugh at that. But if the camera zoomed out and now we see that the window is on the second floor and that the man outside is wearing long stilts, then it becomes a funny picture.

If you cast your minds back to all the costume sketches that were done on TV by comedy double acts or comics using feeds you'll recall how contrast was used to get the funny man his big laugh on entering. The straight man always came on first wearing an immaculate version of whatever costume the sketch called for. Then the comedian followed with a very tatty version of the same costume. If it called for khaki shorts they'd be too long and baggy. The hat would be too large and keep falling over his eyes . . . his sword would be ridiculously long and trip him up each time he moved . . . and so on. The comedy picture was there because the writer, with the aid of the wardrobe department, had first established the norm with the straight man and then deviated from it for the comedian's attire.

Not only can what one wears be funny, but also the way one wears it. I had personal experience of this the day I attended the first read-through of one of my sketches. A coin dropped through the hole in my trousers pocket. I bent down to pick it up and heard a ripping sound. The seat of my trousers had split.

I quickly sat down to hide my embarrassment and would gladly have stayed in that position through the session, but it was not to be. Tommy Cooper, the star of the show, wasn't sure what I meant in describing one bit of funny business, so the producer asked me to act it out for him.

It's one of those things you laugh about afterwards, but at the time my face was all shades of red as I deliberately contrived my movements to avoid ever having to turn my back on the eight people seated round that table. The piece got more laughs than expected and led me to write a subsequent sketch which both Dave King and Dick Emery performed on British television and I later sold to ten different countries.

The simple premise of the sketch was a man expecting a young lady round for a drink and a nice, quiet, pleasant evening. But as he goes to open the door to let her in, he sneezes. And his trouser belt snaps. The rest of the six minute sketch was just his frantic attempts to carry food, drinks and even to dance without his trousers falling down. Pure visual comedy that had the audiences howling with laughter because they knew something the girl in the sketch didn't. They were laughing at the comedian's awkward movements and near disasters as he just managed to keep retaining what dignity he could muster.

Theatrical pantomimes have long given us the humour of men dressing up as women to play the Dame or Ugly Sisters. Comedians Les Dawson, Stanley Baxter, Benny Hill and Ronnies Corbett and Barker do this well. But I also think that female impersonators Danny La Rue and Hinge and Brackett do it too well to be as funny. They dress authentically and don't utilise the fact that outlandish clothes make the characters funnier.

Morecambe and Wise and other comedians have done sketches

which relied on them coming on in the wrong costumes. The writer would qualify it by having them think they were doing say, *Gone With The Wind* and not knowing it had been changed to *Mutiny On The Bounty*. That incongruity of a Yankee soldier on a British ship is played to the full for laughs. The funniest version was probably when the comedian thought he was doing a Yukon sketch and came on dressed up like an eskimo when the sketch being played was Beau Geste set in the hot desert.

Comedian Sid Caesar did a funny sketch where he was chairman at a very important board meeting and entered dressed as a gorilla. The explanation was that he had been to a fancy dress party the night before and the zip had stuck on the costume so he could not get out of it. Seeing a man discussing serious high finance business while dressed like that set the scene for big laughs.

Another way clothing provides comedy is in the sketch where a man and wife have a row and he says he's leaving her for good. But he accidentally gets his jacket cuff button caught in the lace of her dress. Despite his dialogue about going, he is stuck to her and can't leave. Having a stage hand try to surreptitiously creep in with a pair of scissors adds to the fun.

The examples given so far all needed a certain amount of dialogue. But I suppose the purest of comedy is where no dialogue is needed at all. It is obvious to the viewer what is going on. Here is a quickie from *The Dave Allen Show* that had no words spoken.

The Set: A Children's Boating Pond

Four boys (or men dressed as boys) are standing spaced round the pond. Each has a string in his hand, the other end of which is attached to their toy yachts in the water.

One by one we see the yachts keel over and sink. Each time we cut to a close up of its astonished owner to show his angry reaction.

After the fourth yacht has sunk, the camera pulls back so that we see for the first time, a man in a German naval uniform. He is holding a string too. He pulls his string in and we can clearly see that attached to it is a toy submarine. He picks up the submarine and, with a smug expression on his face, goose-steps off.

There is visual comedy that, though not needing dialogue, does nevertheless rely on sound. Like this:

> *A distinguished looking conductor in white tie and tails is facing the camera with baton swinging in his hand as though conducting a full orchestra. (The camera represents the orchestra.)*
>
> *We hear the tail end of a beautiful symphony. The conductor nods appreciatively to camera as though to the musicians. Then he turns to the blacked out area behind him as though facing his audience. He raises his baton and conducts their applause.*
>
> *Under his direction they applaud in a recognisable version of 'Tales from the Vienna Woods.'*

Sometimes, when the tag to a quickie relies on the audience reading some words, it is safer to have the comedian actually read the words out aloud so the audience don't miss it. For instance:

> *The Set: A Library*
>
> *Comedian has his neck bent as he looks along a low middle shelf for a particular book. He carries on right to the end of the row before his facial expression shows he's found the book he wants. He pulls out the book and the camera focuses on its title.*
>
> *Comedian: (Reading Title)* 'How to cure a stiff neck.'
>
> *Camera pulls out for a wider shot to see the Comedian walking away with his neck still bent crooked.*

In that case he said the line for extra insurance. But here's one visual quickie in which the single line of dialogue is so essential that none of the visual part would mean anything without it. It's one Bob Block wrote for British comedian Les Dawson:

> *The Set: Top of the Staircase of a House*

Les creeps as silently as possible up the stairs. He is carrying an enormous burden over his shoulder. Large cloth is draped over the thing he is carrying. The only clue we have is a huge fish sticking out at one end.

He staggers into the bathroom with it and as he passes the camera we can see that it is obviously a large shark with the recognisable fin at the top.

A second later we hear a loud splash. Then Les returns with the empty cloth. He calls down the stairs in a sweet tone:

Les: Darling, tell your mother her bath water's ready.

At the other extreme, here's a quickie with lots of dialogue but which would die without the very important visual bit that it hinges on.

Open on door with notice 'Avis Publishing Company'

Mix through to interior of boardroom. Round the table are four men being addressed by the Chairman:

Chairman: Gentlemen, this year has been a landmark in the history of Avis Publishing Company. We have managed to corner the market in murder stories. And, furthermore, this next year promises . . .

The phone rings — Chairman picks it up listens for a second.

Chairman: (To phone) Darling, I asked you not to call me when I'm working.

We hear an indistinguishable woman's voice talking fast and furiously from the other end of the phone. The Chairman manages to slip in an occasional 'Yes dear' and 'No dear'.

Then, as he continues listening to her, he ties the phone wire into a slip knot and slowly tightens it so that we hear the wife's voice gradually choking at the other end of the phone till it finally stops altogether.

The Chairman puts the phone down and continues his address as though nothing had happened.

Chairman: . . . Next year promises to be an even better year with sales increasing . . . *(Fade out as he continues speaking)*

* * *

I'd like you to glance through these comic thoughts:

An old couple asleep in bed and both have a glass of water on their bedside table with their teeth in. And, at the foot of the bed, is their dog asleep with its teeth in a glass. (Or it would be funny to see a huge glass with two tusks in beside a sleeping elephant.)

Talking of animals — wouldn't it be a funny picture if a skunk approached a well-dressed man, held its tail up like a revolver and said: 'This is a stink-up!'

Suppose you had a convict being visited by his wife and then talking to each other through the wire netting. They soon run out of conversation. He says, 'I can't think of a thing to say.' She says, 'Neither can I. Then shall we . . . ?' He nods, 'Yes' and she takes out a shuttlecock and they start to play badminton over the top of the wire mesh.

The driver of a van with the words 'Novelty Company' on the side is seen squirting water from the carnation in his button-hole into the van's battery.

The driver of a mobile library uses a stack of books as a jack for his van.

A Playboy Bunny waits in the queue at the vet's surgery.

Sign on tall cliff: 'Lovers Leap'. Sign on a short cliff: 'Just Friends Leap'.

A gay wedding with two groom figures on top of the wedding cake.

91

A doctor says, 'I'll be glad when my stethoscope's repaired' and we see that he is listening to a patient's chest through an empty wine glass.

Busty secretary tells her new boss, 'I'm all thumbs.' He says, 'Not from where I'm standing, you're not.'

A man painting a racing stripe on his tortoise's shell.

Father answers front door to robot and shouts back to his daughter, 'Helen, your computer date's arrived.'

Boss dictates to secretary in empty room. Both are sitting on the floor. 'Memo to all personnel re pilfering of office supplies.'

A flat-chested girl goes into a taxidermist's shop, and leaves full-bosomed.

The annual dinner of the Peeping Toms Society — where all the men watch the stripper cabaret through keyholes.

Think sign in yoga school is hung upside down.

Man handing wife a funeral wreath, 'Well, you keep complaining that I never bring you flowers.'

Actor holding girl in arms looks to pit for lines and sees prompter who holds girl in his arms reading the script.

Castaway to another about mermaid: 'Wow! 38-24 and 75p a pound'.

Sexy half-nude girl leaves prisoner's cell and tells guards, 'You can call off the execution. His last request killed him.'

Eskimo child in igloo to father who is reading him *Little Jack Horner:* 'What's a corner?'

Wife to man in bed with feet on pillow: 'All right then — sulk.'

Man in dinner suit to store's complaints manager: 'I'd like to register a formal complaint.'

Judge spinning roulette wheel, to man: 'For illegal gambling, I hereby sentence you to . . .'

Wife and lover are in nude as her husband comes in and sees them. Lover says, 'Would you believe a plague of locusts?'

Man about another man carrying a blank protest banner: 'He's from the Silent Majority.'

Doctor orders barrow boy selling apples to move his barrow from outside the doctor's surgery.

Vet holding stiff snake: 'I'm taking him off starches.'

Soldier has tied string to bad tooth and other end to mortar shell he is about to fire.

Wife holds out bra and asks husband: 'Got a light?'

Man stares at dirty tablecloth in restaurant and says to waitress: 'Say, the spaghetti looks good today.'

Man goes for examination by doctor. Doctor taps man's knee and his foot kicks doctor in the head. Positions are now reversed and man ends up examining ill doctor.

Dutch boy sticks finger in hole in leaky water bed.

Sign on Echo Canyon: 'If You Get No Answer — Try Again In Five Minutes.'

As monk glares, nurse with huge hypodermic needle tells doctor: 'He just broke his vow of silence.'

Chauffeur driving boss, holds car phone and says: 'Hold on — I'll see if he's in.'

Nurse to patient completely bandaged except for one eye: 'If you need anything, just wink.'

Boss to pregnant dance teacher: 'What happened to your sense of rhythm?'

Kangaroo with bandaged foot hops on pogo stick.

Man to wife wearing low cut gown: 'I sure hope you don't get the hiccups.'

Those cartoon type gags all relied on the visual pictures that were described. None of them was meant for television. They are just examples of how to get comedy out of visual pictures. And the main lesson to be learnt from them was that you don't need any actual drawings or photographs. The words alone are sufficient for you to conjure up the pictures in your own minds.

That's because I didn't mention anything you weren't already familiar with. I didn't talk about my Uncle Charlie, whom you've never seen, or refer to a building or film or play or species of animal that you might not know. If I had done, then you would not be able to conjure up in your minds the same picture as I'd thought of and our lines of communication on that particular gag would be lost.

It would be like my talking in a language that you didn't understand.

So the essential thing when writing visual comedy into a script is to use descriptions the reader will immediately be able to recognise. If you are describing a fat woman it's no use saying she had the kind of figure that made Tessie O'Shea look like Pat Coombs if the sketch is destined for a foreign market where both these ladies are unknown. You couldn't say the character had a Jimmy Edwards moustache or was Ronnie Corbett's height. Or had the personality of Nicholas Parsons . . . the charm of Bernard Manning . . . the diction of Arthur Mullard . . . the sincerity of Hughie Green . . . or the singing voice of Terry Wogan. Those last five descriptions are facetious, but unless the reader knows Nicholas Parsons, Bernard Manning, Arthur Mullard, Hughie Green and Terry Wogan they'd be lost on him.

Perhaps the best thing I could do here is give you some examples of visual quickies that have been performed on television here or abroad and let you see for yourself how they looked in script form:

Vibrating Machine Quickie

Int.   Living Room.   Day

Man is using one of these vibrating machines with the wide belt round the back that shakes you about.

Man: (To wife) I'm glad you bought this machine, Gladys. It's great. So relaxing.
Wife: I'm pleased you like it. Had enough?
Man: No, I could stay on this all day.
Wife: (Looks at watch) You can't, Bert. Your lunch hour's over. Time you got back to work.
Man: Yeah, I suppose you're right.

He turns machine off . . . undoes the belt . . . goes off camera and brings back road drill.

Man: (Going to work) See you later, luv! (Blackout)

* * *

Hitch-Hiker Quickie

Ext. Motorway. Day.

Comedian is driving car. Camera is inside car as it approaches the start of the motorway. This is so we can see the action from the Comedian's point of view.

A Man is at the side of the road trying to thumb a lift. Comedian sees him, shakes his head, and drives on.

About ten yards up the road there is another Man also thumbing a lift. Once again the Comedian shakes his head and drives on.

This happens again with a third Man who gets the same reaction from the Comedian.

Twenty yards further up the road there is a very attractive young lady trying to thumb a lift. Comedian sees her. He reacts eagerly and screeches the car to a sudden halt.

He gets out and opens the passenger side door for the young lady to get in. Then he gets back in the car himself and drives off.

A few seconds later the girl starts to lift her skirt a little. This attracts the Comedian's attention and he stares at her thigh.

The young lady raises her skirt even further and we see that she has a small revolver attached to her tights.

She pulls out the revolver and points it threateningly at the Comedian and mimes ordering him out of the car.

He stops the car and gets out. She moves over to the driving seat and drives off.

The Comedian moves to the side of the road and (like the other three men) jerks his thumb trying to hitch a lift.

*   *   *

Snake Charmer Quickie

Set: An Empty Stage.   Day.

An Indian snake charmer sits in front of a basket and mimes playing the flute. We hear the flute music.

Gradually we see the snake rising from inside the basket. (Pulled up by hidden wire).

Comedian enters also dressed as a snake charmer. He sits down in front of a second basket. He mimes playing the flute. We hear jazzed up flute music.

This time, instead of the snake rising, the Comedian slowly rises up and up till he is out of the picture. (Comedian is, of course, on a hidden wire too).

*   *   *

Bathroom Quickie by Bob Bass.

The Set: Int.   Bathroom.   Day.

Naked woman is in the bath with the water up to her shoulders.

Fireman enters the bathroom looking for the fire.

96

*When he sees the woman he shields his eyes and
backs out of the bathroom.*

*Two seconds later he re-enters, smiling and carrying
a stirrup pump.*

*He places the suction end of the pump into the
bath and starts to pump.*

*The woman, realising what the fireman is trying
to do, turns on both the taps.*

The fireman pumps faster and faster.

*   *   *

Football Match Quickie by Vivien Bryson.

The Set: Exterior.   Football Pitch.   Day.

*A football match is in progress. Comedian is the
very officious referee.*

*He spots what he thinks is a foul and blows his
whistle.*

*He goes over to the player who argues with him.
Comedian takes out his pencil and notebook and
writes down player's name and cautions him.*

Then he whistles for game to continue.

Fade out.

Fade in again later.

The Set: Outside the Football Ground.   Day.

*Comedian, now dressed in street clothes, is about
to get into his car parked by the kerb.*

There is a whistle.

Comedian looks round and sees the player whose name he took down, standing there in his police uniform.

Player points to double yellow lines that the car is parked on.

He has great satisfaction in taking out his notepad and pencil and writing down Comedian's name to book him for illegal parking.

*　*　*

Comedians' Canteen Quickie.

Int. Section of Canteen. Day.

Comedian holds tray and carries it along in front of glass cubby holes labelled with various foods.

He stops by one marked 'Grapefruit'. He lifts the glass and takes out portion of grapefruit.

He moves along to cubby hole marked 'Coq au Vin'. Lifts glass and takes out chicken dish.

Then he moves further along to cubby hole marked 'Pies'. There are several choices and he selects the one marked 'Custard'.

He lifts the glass and a custard pie is pushed through into his face.

Those, written mostly by former students of mine, are quickies that scored because they were completely visual and easy to understand.

*　*　*

Benny Hill specialises in what's called the 'optical illusion' gag. He would have a man standing in a park and there'd be a hose watering the flowers. But from the angle of the shot it appears that the man is peeing. Benny bounces a white beach ball which gets lost behind a hedge. A short-skirted girl bends down to pick up something from the ground. He mistakes her white-knickered bottom for the ball and gets slapped round the face. Or he'd do a William Tell act and fire an arrow at the apple on top of a busty girl's head. Instead the arrow hits her in the chest which deflates with a hissing noise. These are the kind of visual gags that have made Benny Hill one of the highest paid comics around today. His edited shows are now being shown on American TV and sold to about forty-two countries.

Tommy Cooper gets lots of visual laughs by doing his magic tricks badly. The late Dick Emery got visual laughs when he played his female characters Mandy, Hetty and the Duchess. If a real woman did it it wouldn't be funny. Dick also got laughs with the slipping teeth of the vicar he portrayed. And the banging on the deaf aid of the Old Colonel character. All well observed characters that got more laughs for how they looked and acted than what they actually said.

Red Skelton used to start off all his TV shows with a short mime spot. Not a word said except for the introduction in setting up the situation. He did a beautifully thought out three minute bit on a golfer playing in a very high wind and being blown away from the ball every time he tried to hit it. Then when he had managed to anchor himself in position, the wind direction changed and the ball was being blown away from him. So he anchored the ball down by tying it to a huge boulder and when he finally hit it it bounced off the boulder and hit him in the eye. But we never saw the boulder, the ball, or Red's golfclub except in our own imagination. It was all expertly mimed.

In another mime I saw Skelton play a tramp on a park bench who saw half a dollar on the ground and just as he was about to reach out and pick it up other people started to walk by. He went through three or four minutes trying to find excuses for being down on all fours as he searched for the half dollar that one of the passers-by accidentally kicked into the grass.

A few years ago, Peter Dulay and I wrote the Dutch TV entry for the Golden Rose Festival which was all silent. It ran for about forty minutes and was all camera tricks that could be done with the Chroma Key (sometimes known as blue separation) system. It was called blue separation originally because at that time only the colour blue could be used. Now several different colours can be used. What happens is that you shoot the scene against a huge screen of one plain colour. On that screen you can put up any scene you like just as if it was back projection. But if the screen were blue then anything you wear of that same colour becomes invisible. If I were dressed from neck to toes in the same tone of blue as the screen then you'd see right through my body and just my head would be visible.

We did one sequence of about two minutes with just two fellows playing table tennis. At one point we used a blue ball so it appeared as though they were rushing to and fro hitting nothing. We gave one of them a blue bat then later the other a blue bat so they seemed to be hitting the ball with nothing . . . We dressed one of the players in blue so that he disappeared entirely but the ball was still being hit back from his side. At one point we used a blue table and so made the table disappear. The overall picture was funny and got a lot of laughs, as did the other trick camera gimmicks we used in the show.

I remember another show that same year at Montreux which had a very funny sketch based on a simple premise. It was a dentist who had to give his patient an injection that would make his mouth area completely numb in a matter of seconds. But just as he was about to administer the injection, he sneezed and injected the needle into his own arm instead. The dentist going through that tooth extraction scene with one limp arm was hilarious. He had to invent lots of different ways of holding the instruments he couldn't otherwise have even lifted off the trolley.

If I were asked which visual comedy scenes stuck out most in my memory, I would surely place the chewing gum factory scene in the film *The Adventures of Rabbi Jacob* as top of the list. And the scene from the old silent Harry Langdon film where he threw stones at the policeman. Both very funny and each based on a simple set up, That fourteen minute scene of solid laughs in the *Rabbi Jacob* film was a cops and robbers chase through a chewing gum factory where all the people involved got stuck in the chewing gum. The chase that started off at a fast pace ended in slow motion as they had to drag each foot off the floor for every step because they kept being stuck. They stuck to everything they touched. If the film comes round your way again, don't miss it.

The Harry Langdon scene started with him being moved on by a policeman for loitering. He sees a dummy policeman prop being placed outside the stage door of a theatre and vents his anger by pelting it with stones from all different angles. Then, as he turns to find more stones, the dummy is taken inside the theatre and a real policeman comes along and decides to sit in that same place for a rest. But Harry doesn't know this and continues to have fun throwing the stones. It was the policeman's reaction and then Harry's realisation when what he thinks is the dummy, starts to come alive and chase him that made me laugh so loud at the time.

Slapstick is the most universal of all comedy forms. You've all seen the kind of sketch where the comedian would set out to do a simple thing like wallpapering the living room, and get himself into a heck of a mess. Paste would be sloshed all over him and his helpers and on the floor too. They'd end up slipping and sliding into each other causing more and more havoc all the time. That, together with the traditional custard pie and banana skin, is all part of the very broad comedy we call slapstick.

Once you start these sketches they seem to write themselves because most of them are based on a chain reaction. You just plant the first seed and the rest is a natural sequence of events. Let's take a fashionable party where the nobility and aristocracy are gathered to honour a man who had just returned from ten years on safaris into the African jungle. The party would be going along quite well until the man's aide (our comedian), suddenly discovers that the tarantula they brought back for the zoo is not in its box. It shouldn't be hard to imagine the chaos that would follow. People would be panic-stricken and run in all directions, bumping into waiters laden with trays of food and drinks. Someone's hairpiece would fall off and be mistaken for the large venomous spider and be squirted with soda water to keep it at bay. So when its owner put it back on, it would have shrunk and would look ridiculous. A fat woman would back into something sharp like a pencil point and think that she had been bitten in the rear by the tarantula and that she was dying. There are no end of things you can find to fit into this kind of situation. But the most important part of the sketch would occur right at the beginning. Because in order for this to be really funny, the audience need to know that the comedian had looked into the wrong box and that the spider hadn't escaped at all, that all this panic and chaos and damage was unnecessary.

What I'm trying to say is that all slapstick must have a reason. Slapstick without a legitimate reason is just plain silly. Laurel and Hardy would never have thrown custard pies at each other without a good reason. Something would have happened to motivate the action. A typical situation would have the fat one, Hardy, alone in a bakery shop in which the display shelves were lined with custard pies. In bending down to tie his shoelace, his large posterior would hit something which in turn hit something else that hit something else, too, in the chain reaction. It would finally cause one of the custard pies to fall off the top shelf and score a direct hit on Hardy, splattering all over his face. At that very moment Laurel would walk in and see his partner's face covered in the custard and he'd laugh. So, when Hardy clears the custard from his eyes, the first thing he sees is his partner laughing and immediately assumes he threw the pie. He retaliates by throwing a pie at Laurel. This annoys Laurel who throws one back at him. And so the war of pies develops as other customers walk into the shop and get involved. Both men threw their first pie in, they thought, retaliation to the one they received. The slapstick, therefore, had a legitimate excuse.

And though we all laugh when we see the comedian or villain slip on a banana skin or fall down an open manhole, the writer has prepared us for it. He has planted the banana skin or manhole and cleverly contrived the situation so that we will want that person to suffer the indignity of the fall. And that is the important key to it all. It has to happen to the person we want it to. If your mother or sister fell down a coalhole you wouldn't laugh, you'd be more concerned about their health. But you may not feel the same if the victim were your mother-in-law or your boss or the income tax inspector. You would be more likely to say, 'Serves them right. They got their come-uppance.' So, in writing this kind of sketch, your victim should be the big bully getting his come-uppance.

For good examples of how slapstick works, you might try watching circus clowns in action. You'll see how one or other of the clowns sets out to inflict some injury or indignity on the others and gets it himself instead. He has made himself the villain by wanting to do it to the others and we, the viewers, feel it only just that it should happen to him.

6 / Situation Comedy I: Characterisation

Good writing, whether it be for comedy or drama, is reliant on strong character delineation. Think of the great comedy stars like Jack Benny, Schnozzle Durante, Groucho Marx, Woody Allen, Buster Keaton, Charlie Chaplin and W. C. Fields. All so easy to impersonate and recognise because of their traits and physical appearance.

Jack Benny had the effeminate walk; the blank stare; the

violin playing; and the imaginary toupet. His character traits included his stinginess; the touchiness about his age; and his readiness to play the violin at any and every opportunity. Benny's four long-time writers Sam Perrin, George Balzer, Hal Goldman and Al Gordon built their boss's character to the point where he just had to walk into any given situation and we immediately knew what his reactions would be. That's good writing.

Guests invited to a Jack Benny party at his home knew they were expected to not only bring a present, but also two dollars to park their car in his front garden. And they'd also bring earplugs because they knew that the words 'Top International Cabaret' on the invitation meant that Jack would be playing his violin.

Jack Benny would scramble over all manner of deliberately planted mines and other booby traps to borrow things from his next door neighbour. He even risked his life this way on one occasion just to borrow a single egg because the local grocery store wouldn't sell him less than half a dozen at a time. And he'd heard a rumour that the price of eggs was going down by the end of the week.

He borrowed so much that, in one show the neighbour came over to Benny's house to borrow back his toothbrush. He looked round the lounge and said, 'Jack, you've got so much of my stuff here that I feel more at home in your place than I do in my own.'

Schnozzle Durante's physical characteristics weren't hard to spot. He had the size of nose that made him taller lying down than he was standing up. He claimed to have got fan mail from anteaters. And that eskimoes looked upon him as a Casanova. He once cracked that he was going to have a nose bob, but they couldn't find an operating table long enough.

As a character you could sum him up as a genial simpleton who sang songs punctuated with gags. And that he had problems pronouncing words with more than one syllable. Instead of Muchas Gracias he'd say Muchus Gracious. Cockles of your heart became Cocktails of your heart. Like Jack Benny's parsimony, Durante's stock-in-trade was his Malapropisms. In his famous song *I'm Durante the Patron of the Arts* he refers to the operas *Tales of the Vienna Rolls . . . Madame Buttermilk . . . The Sextette from Leechee Nuts . . .* and *The Quartet From Rigor Mortis*.

His writers had him describe himself as having 'a good deal of cheek — and a hell of a lot of nose.' 'My trouble is I gotta winning smile, but a losing face.' At a formal affair he said, 'I wear a tuxedo to all the concerts now. I used to wear tails, but they made me look lumpy. How was I to know you're not supposed to tuck them inside your trousers?'

Most of Durante's knocking gags were aimed at himself to show his humility, but occasionally he'd allow himself a mild attempt at insulting a guest. Like the time he said of a well known fat comedian, 'He used to be a cowboy but he found it too difficult working in the Middle West. He had too much middle to fit in the West.' But then Schnozzle would even mollify that by adding, 'Me and my big mouth! I'd get rid of it only it's such a handy place to keep my teeth.' He was like a cuddly teddy bear who could never annoy or frustrate anyone.

British comedian Harry Worth could surely also be described as a genial simpleton, but he was different from Durante. Worth, in character, certainly could — and did — annoy and frustrate anybody in officialdom that tried to have a sensible conversation with him.

It would be believable for Harry Worth to fill up his basket with goods at the supermarket and then knock at the manager's office and ask for the money to pay for them. The bemused manager would tell Harry that the bank is down the road and Harry would reply, 'I know that, I'm not a fool. But you're the one who's got my money.' 'Me? Why me?' 'Well,' explains Harry, believing entirely in what he is about to say, 'I've been shopping in this store for two years now. And every week I've bought things here that had notices saying SAVE 3p or SAVE 4p or SAVE 9p. I've worked it out that up till now I've saved £26 in this store. And I want to collect some of it now to pay for these groceries.'

In essence Harry Worth could be described as the male counterpart to the beloved Gracie Allen. Both trod the thin line between innocence and banality. And their writers knew full well that if the characters ever did get banal they would completely lose their believability and charm.

It would be useful to give you an example of what would be going too far. Let's imagine that we make Harry Worth a policeman in one story. This is a standard situation that new writers often choose. They have the comedian witness a jewellery store robbery where the crook throws a brick through the plate glass window and grabs the rings, necklaces, watches, etc., on display. Harry arrests the man, points to the broken glass scattered on the ground and charges him with littering the pavement. The gag being that he had completely overlooked the more serious charge of robbery. That would be making the comedian unbelievably daft.

The right way to treat that situation from the Harry Worth

angle would be something along these lines. There would be two crooks, one with a camera. They would explain to Harry that they were from the BBC or any other TV network, and were shooting a documentary about the appalling rise in the crime rate. Their job was to demonstrate how a crime is committed. Then they actually carry out the crime with Harry Worth not only not interfering, but actively helping them by holding back any other people that might try to stop them. He'd tell any onlookers, 'Don't worry, folk, it's just a film.'

Tommy Cooper is another genial simpleton, but with a different approach as far as writing situations for him are concerned. His strength lies in his facial reactions and complete bewilderment rather than in lots of dialogue. You see, while Harry Worth can create a situation, it is best for Tommy Cooper to walk into a situation that others have created and mistake what is going on.

If he was walking along a hotel corridor and heard someone being murdered in one of the rooms, he'd call the police, the ambulances and even the fire brigade to break the door down. And the comedy would come from the fact that we know that there is just a baby in a cot in there with the TV set left on so that it wouldn't feel left alone. The murder scene obviously (obvious to us but not to Tommy) coming from the TV set. This can be milked for laughs by intercutting the scenes on the TV. Let us say that it is a *Starsky and Hutch* show on TV and the scenes alternate between the attempted murder and an attempted seduction scene between Hutch and a girlfriend. So one moment Tommy will hear a woman screaming and the next time he goes back it's kissing and purring . . . and when he goes back to the door again he hears screaming once more . . . and so on. Tommy's reaction of 'I wish they'd make up their mind' would be funny. But the main humour of the situation comes from the fact that we know something that Tommy doesn't. That is usually the best premise for a Tommy Cooper situation.

An interesting and/or funny character in a situation comedy relies heavily on what you give him to say and do. Often the actor or director will add an extra touch, but basically the problem is yours. You have to describe that character in the dialogue and action so vividly that we know *who* and *what* he is and how he goes about his daily life.

Here is a brief excerpt from a series called *Birds Eye View* starring Millicent Martin as an air stewardess. I chose it because it very quickly sets up the three main characters and their relationship to each other. The series was shot in England but made by an American TV company so the script is laid out American style.

Fade in:
1. *Ext. London.   Day.*
   Establishing Shots of several famous landmarks.

2. *Ext. London Street.   Day.*
   Heavy traffic, featuring a taxi.

3. *Close on Taxi.*
   We find Millie and Maggie in the back seat. They are dressed in their stewardess uniforms.

4. *Ext. Sky.   Day.*
   A jetliner at extremely low altitude. Camera pans down to frame airport entrance. The taxi pulls into shot, stops and Millie and Maggie get out, each carrying a small suitcase. They pay the driver and enter the terminal.

5. *Int. Terminal.   Day.*
   Millie and Maggie cross, passing an airline information counter, behind which sits a girl. They wave at her. She beckons to them. They go to the counter.

Girl

Beauchamp wants to see you.

The girls, who had been smiling, now look concerned.

Millie

Was he smiling?

Maggie

Are you kidding? The last time he smiled was when the Nazis marched on Poland.

Girl

He just said he wanted to see you as soon as you came in.

Millie

Thanks, luv.

Millie and Maggie turn and continue walking across the large floor.

6. *Int. Airlines Office.   Day.*
Millie and Maggie approach a door marked: 'Elliot Beauchamp, Supervisor of Stewardess Personnel.' Millie knocks.

> Beauchamp (o.s.)
Come.

Millie opens the door and they go in.

7. *Int. Beauchamp's Office.   Day.*
Beauchamp stands behind his desk. He's a middle-aged man who looks as though his chief pleasure in life is reading the fine print.

> Beauchamp
Sit.

Millie and Maggie each take a chair facing the desk. After they are seated, Beauchamp sits — a very precise operation. He indicates two file-folders lying on the desk.

> Beauchamp
> (Continuing)
Do you know what these are?

Millie and Maggie shake their heads.

> Beauchamp
> (Continuing)
These are personnel records. To be exact, they are the personnel records of Margaret Ralston (*nods to Maggie*) and Millicent Grover (*nods to Millie*). I wish to read you several items of interest from these records. (*Opens one, reads*). Margaret Ralston.

8. *Shot.   Maggie.*
as Beauchamp goes on.

> Beauchamp (v.o.)
Age: 28. Born: San Francisco, California. Employed by this airline for eleven months, under the exchange programme with our American affiliate. During that

period, reported seventeen times for infractions of company rules.

9. *Back to scene*
   Beauchamp puts down Maggie's file and picks up the other.

10. *Shot.   Millie.*

> *Beauchamp*
> Millicent Grover. Age: 27.

> *Millie*
> 28, sir. I had a birthday last week.

> *Beauchamp (v.o.)*
>   (flat)
> Happy birthday. Age: *28*. Born: London, England.

> *Millie*
> You see, Mr Beauchamp, it wasn't really London, but just outside of it. But nobody ever heard of the place, so I always say London.

> *Beauchamp (v.o.)*
>   (clears throat, then)
> Born: *London*. Employed by this airline eleven months . . . .

> *Millie*
> Actually, it's 49 weeks — a little over eleven months.

> *Beauchamp (v.o.)*
> 49 weeks. During this period, also reported for seventeen infractions of company rules. Do you agree with *that*, Miss Grover?

> *Millie*
> Yes, sir. Seventeen — right on the button.

11. *Back to scene.*

> *Beauchamp*
>   (shaking head)
> Seventeen infractions. All the more remarkable in light of the fact there are only *eighteen* company rules. Save

for setting fire to an airplane, you two have broken every one.

Millie
We'll try harder, Mr Beauchamp, honestly we will.

Beauchamp
Yes, you will. Hundreds of young women from all over the world want to work for this airline. If you don't improve, two of them will get a chance. That's all.

Nodding, Millie and Maggie get up and exit.

Dissolve.

Comedy actor Peter Jones played the part of Beauchamp and from that short excerpt we knew that he would be chasing them up on every little thing they did. Ready to dismiss them immediately he caught them infringing even the smallest company rule. So all the writers had to do is put them into situations where, in order to help other people, they would have to break a rule. And the comedy came from their frantic attempts to hide it from Beauchamp.

In that one line about Beauchamp, 'The last time he smiled was when the Nazis marched on Poland', we got a good insight into what he was going to be like. It is a ploy often used by writers to describe a character through the eyes of others in the show.

Here's another way of doing that. This time the script is laid out for British television.

Opening titles.

Then . . . Fade in on:

Int. Kitchen/Dining Room. Morning.

It is the home of Bryan and Susan Tyndall. They're a middle-aged married couple. They are seated across the table from one another over breakfast. Susan is reading a woman's magazine and Bryan is reading the morning paper.

There's a third place set at the table, but the seat is empty.

Susan: (Looks up at wall clock) Roy's late down this morning.

Bryan: (Interrupted from reading) What did you say?

Susan: Roy's down late this morning.

Bryan: Good. I can have my breakfast in peace for once. I don't have to watch that brother of yours stuffing his gullet with all those pills and medicines and capsules he keeps taking.

Susan: (Puts her magazine down) It's not Roy's fault. He's delicate. He can't help being ill.

Bryan: Susan, I've told you a hundred times — your brother's just a hypochondriac. That boy isn't ill here *(Points to stomach)* — he's sick, here. *(Points to head)* He's nutty as a fruitcake. He's convinced himself he's got everything in the medical book. Even the ruddy footnotes.

Susan: Oh Bryan, stop exaggerating.

Bryan: (Puts down newspaper) Who's exaggerating? That boy keeps four chemist shops going on his own. Have you seen his wardrobe upstairs? It's stacked high with pills for headache, backache, stomach ache, colic, hard pad, athlete's foot and I shouldn't be surprised if he hasn't got some there for ingrowing toenail. There's even a whole drawer filled with nothing but indigestion pills. And he only needs those because he swallows the others too quickly.

Susan: You're not being fair. Roy *is* ill.

Bryan: He is not. He's just got himself a built-in excuse for not getting involved in any physical activity . . . such as work!

Susan: Roy wants to work. I know he does.

Bryan: Then how do you explain his being fired from no less than seven jobs in the past four weeks? Answer me that!

Susan: He just hasn't had the right one yet. He's trying to find himself.

Bryan: Good. And while he's looking he can find himself another place to live. I'm throwing him out.

Susan: But Bryan, he's my brother.

Bryan: I don't care if he's your second cousin twice removed. I'm running a house here, not a home for the perpetually unemployed. The reason

he can't hold a job is because he's pig ignorant.
Susan: Well he can't help that.
Bryan: Of course he could. He could go to the library and bury his head in a book occasionally instead of staying here burying it under a towel with Friars Balsam.
Susan: Give him another chance. He's got a job to go to this morning. Maybe he'll stick to this one.
Bryan: There's no maybe about it this time, Susan. If he loses this job he loses his bed and board here an' all. And that's final.

Roy enters at the end of that last speech. He is thirty years old, five foot eight, thin build and wears steel rimmed glasses.

Roy: (Smiles) Good morning.
Bryan: (Sarcastically) It *was.*

In that bit of script we got a full picture of what Roy was going to be like before we ever set eyes on him. And he only has to live up to the things Bryan said about him to be funny.

From that scene we've learned that he is under the threat of eviction if he doesn't hold on to the job he is about to go to. So the writer has to find a job for him that he would have to desperately try to hang on to. And if it is one that requires someone with perfect health then Roy would have to bluff his way through it. Taking his regular pills and medicines as secretly as possible. Can you imagine him, for instance, getting a job as physical instructor at a health farm? I'm sure you can find your own ideas for jobs that would be alien to his natural inclinations, and so be funny. But the object of this example was to show how to set up his character.

* * *

How do you find characters for your situation comedy scripts? Well, I recently learned that there's a school of acting in New York that presents its students with a book of pictures of people taken from the daily newspapers. It's something like a police mug-shot book. The students have to select any picture at random and give a description of what they think that person is like. His age, nationality, marital status, job, his good and bad points etc. What sort of situations would please him, or what would make him angry. In other words they build up a whole dossier on a person just from seeing their picture.

I myself often sit in a crowded bus or train and try to imagine what the people around me do for a living and how they conduct themselves where they work and at home. I wonder if that fat lady in the corner has been eating too much because she has worries or is a glutton. Whether that fellow sitting next to her is rolling his own cigarettes because he is short of money. And what might have made him short of money.

Is that well-groomed girl sitting across the aisle on her way to an interview for a job? And is she confident? Or does the fact that she keeps looking at her reflection in the window show that she is worried about her appearance?

That man that travels on my train every morning with his seeing eye dog, I wonder how he feels. How long has he been blind? How does his dog know what station to lead him out on? I was once told that the dog counts the stops and knows to make his move to alight from the train at the sixth stop. But many times the train has stopped along the way when the signal has been red. Does the dog count those stops in as part of the six? And then I start to wonder if the dog has ever led its master out at the wrong station and what were the consequences? Could be the basis for a good story.

If you have an enquiring mind you will have no difficulty in finding good characters and situations for those characters. And it is, of course, the situations you put those characters in that will bring out their traits and characteristics and stamp them as individuals.

Living with a person gives you a greater insight to who and what they are, because you get the chance to witness their actions and reactions under a whole variety of stresses. For instance, you see them angry. It might be over something petty that most people would just laugh off. You may see them as a hypocrite. Someone who perhaps outwardly supports sexual equality yet insists their eighteen-year-old daughter be home by eleven while their seventeen-year-old son can stay out till midnight.

When you are searching for characters for your stories you should live with them in your imagination. In your mind's eye pretend that you're their husband or wife or mother or father or daughter or son. Suppose you, in that role, had a problem and approached them with it, how would they be likely to react? If you wanted to borrow money off them for a holiday they didn't think you needed, would they be sympathetic? Indifferent? Insulting? Would they try to talk you out of the holiday rather than lend you the money? Might they possibly delay a decision in the hope that you'd forget the whole thing?

Probe the nature of your characters well enough to be able to gauge the way they may meet awkward situations. If their car goes wrong on the day after the guarantee expires, would they pretend it happened the previous day and say they could not return with it sooner? Would they query a hefty telephone bill and insist they could not have been so talkative on the phone? What would they do if they found a wallet in the street with money in it? Would they take it to the police or keep it for themselves? If they saw a mugging would they offer to identify the culprit, or play it safe and pretend they hadn't noticed? If a customs official at the airport found a watch they hadn't declared, would they panic and admit their guilt or say they forgot and try to bluff their way out of it?

Does the profession or trade of your character affect him outside working hours? In other words, are there traces of his work in his manner or speech at home? Does a prison officer treat his family at home as though they were all criminals? Does a naval officer talk at home in nautical terms? Or a lawyer in legal jargon? Does a time and efficiency expert complain continually to his wife about her wasting time and money? Does a psychiatrist look for hidden meanings in everything his wife and children say? When vicars get together do they ever exchange dirty jokes? I've always wondered whether the clergy always take the trouble to say grace before every meal. Even the snacks between meals?

Be inquisitive. Keep looking at the people around you and asking questions. Study a book on body language and tune in on a person's attitude as well as what he is saying verbally. It's almost like a lie detector. Income tax inspectors and people conducting job interviews use it all the time.

If you haven't already got Dr Wayne W. Dyer's book *Your Erroneous Zones*, I urge you to get a copy (it's in paperback published by Avon). It's psychology made simple and enjoyable. I recommend it because I found it most helpful in pointing out why personnel officers I know and meet regularly do some of the things they do. It explains the fears and anxieties that motivate their peculiar actions. And I learned that basically they shared my own fears and anxieties, but because they are who they are, they manifested them in their own way.

I don't want to get too heavy on this psychology bit, but it is a subject that fascinates me. And one that has provided me with the tools to make the characters I need for my situation comedies.

114

* * *

Top situation comedy writers will all tell you that their lead
characters, and indeed almost all their characters, are based on
people they themselves knew. A perfect example of this is Alf
Garnett of *Till Death Us Do Part* which later became Archie
Bunker in the American version called *All in the Family*.

Johnny Speight has written all the episodes of *Till Death Us
Do Part* and keeps the Alf Garnett character consistent by
knowing the fellow it's based on. It's Speight's own father. The
series actually came to be written because one day Johnny
Speight was having a drink with two top BBC TV executives
and was telling them about his father who had been very ill.
Speight Senior was a dockworker and extremely bigoted.

The family's doctor was ill too, so his deputy was sent to
make a house call on the bedridden Mr Speight. That deputy
doctor was a black West Indian who quickly diagnosed the illness as being very serious and stayed at the bedside all through
the night administering the necessary treatment to prevent the
man dying. But throughout it all, Johnny's father kept shouting,
'Get this coon's hands off me! Don't let him touch me! His lot
have just come down from the trees, they have!' He kept up this
stream of abuse without ever acknowledging that the man he
was attacking was actually saving his life. Speight Senior, I'm
told, was full of racial intolerance.

Those BBC TV executives saw the funny side of it and
commissioned a pilot script based on that character. Johnny
invented the wife, daughter and son-in-law to complete the
family. But he very carefully wrote these subsidiary characters
so they would contrast with Alf Garnett and thereby highlight
his intolerance and blind hate of anything that wasn't what he
termed 'truly British'.

In Chapter One, I demonstrated that some of the best gags
come out of exaggeration. And, in effect, that same technique
worked with Alf Garnett and Archie Bunker. They had the
same hates and prejudices as many other people, but they were
manifested in a more exaggerated way. Neither of them would
be willing to listen to reason. Their minds are made up before
any argument or debate even starts and nothing would shift
their point of view.

We all know people like that and so, for us the viewers, the
characters rang true. And for the writer, Johnny Speight, it was
consistent because all he had to do was imagine how his own

father would react to a situation and the script virtually wrote itself.

So I would advise you to follow Johnny Speight's example and examine the people around you for the possibility of turning them into situation comedy characters. Take the man who lives next door to you. Let us suppose that he suddenly went missing and you were asked by the police to give as accurate as possible a description of him. What could you tell about him? What's his complexion like? Is he fastidious or careless about his appearance? Does he dress appropriately for his age and position? Does he walk upright or with a stoop or even slovenly?

What about his face? Has he a moustache or beard? If so, what shape is that beard or moustache? What length are his sideburns? Is his neck perhaps scraggy? Is his chin flabby? Does he have a normal chin or is it slightly receding or protruding? How would you describe the shape of his mouth or nose? Is his hair thick, normal or thinning? What exact shade is the colour of his hair? And what shade are the colour of his eyes?

From the physical side we move on to the actual character of the man. For until we know what his character is like we cannot foresee how he will react to any given situation. It's useful to list as many adjectives as you can to measure against the man. Here are some to start you off:

Kind . . . spiteful . . . snobbish . . . loving . . . clever . . . dull . . . sharp . . . boring . . . sympathetic . . . bigoted . . . cunning . . . lazy . . . slovenly . . . careless . . . mean . . . generous . . . philandering . . . shy . . . monosyllabic . . . religious . . . amoral . . . high-principled . . . servile . . . facile . . . narcissistic . . . sexy . . . sycophantic . . . frenetic . . . panicky . . . collected . . . manic-depressive . . . warm . . . restless . . . childish . . . gossipy . . . mischievous . . . square . . . modern . . . with-it . . . freakish . . . two-faced . . . stalwart . . . ingenious . . . selfish . . . selfless . . . loud-mouthed . . . tender . . . regal . . . decisive . . . indecisive . . . shallow . . . awe-inspiring . . . demanding . . . commanding . . . ineffectual . . . overbearing . . . moody . . . cheeky . . . raucous . . . rude . . . brash . . . foolhardy . . . tactful . . . tactless . . . temperamental . . . dishonest . . .

That should be enough to be going on with, but with a bit of thought you could probably double that list. And when you have your completed list, apply them all to your own next door neighbour and see which adjectives describe him accurately as you see him.

Remember that in this writing business people's characters are never completely black or white. They can often fall between two definite descriptions. A shy person might only be shy when he encounters a member of the opposite sex and yet be completely outgoing when dealing with his workmates. A person might be hard and bigoted when his daughter announces she wants to marry someone of a different race or religion and yet be quite friendly with people of that race or religion normally.

Let us suppose that I wanted to write about my own next door neighbour. I'll use some of the points listed above to try to describe him for you so you can see him as I do. He's forty-eight years old, tall, handsome, medium build and has one of those open faces that you would immediately put your trust in. Though not a witty man himself, he is always the first to smile when someone else says something funny.

His name is Peter and he is a senior solicitor's clerk who has all the qualifications to become a fully fledged solicitor, but feels that he is now too old to study three years for the necessary exam. Peter's accent is middle class and so is his mode of living. He owns the four bedroom semi which he shares with his wife and three teenage kids. His political beliefs veer towards socialism, but he seldom discusses it. He believes that a man's politics and religion are his own private business.

Peter's mode of dress is sober, as befits a man in the legal profession. He drives a four-year-old Ford Cortina though he could easily afford something better. It's not because he is stingy, but rather because he feels comfortable with it and has a secret fear of change.

The two dominant things in Peter's life are his work and his family. And it's because these two overlap that he might be a good candidate for a situation comedy series. Like most legal-minded people, Peter has a methodical mind. And that is the stumbling block at home. None of his family are methodical at all. They never put things back where they ought to be or wear the right clothes for the right occasion or act in any way that the text books say they should. While he himself meticulously lives by the letter of the law, Peter's family often carelessly sail pretty close to breaking it.

Monica, that's Peter's wife, gets herself involved with so many different charity committees that she's forever giving away half her living money to needy causes. Everytime Peter saves hard for a new bathroom suite or a foreign holiday, Monica winds up giving the money away to some charity or other. She would be the ideal victim for a confidence trickster.

Their older two children are pop music fans who think their

117

father is a square. Peter does make some attempts to share their interest in modern dancing, but makes such a hash of it that they always laugh at him. The youngest child, just thirteen, is a football enthusiast who supports the Arsenal football club while Peter himself favours the rival Tottenham Hotspurs.

So the conflict from which I could draw most of the comedy is the contrast between Peter, the respected and very competent, orderly, solicitor's clerk, and the hopeless battle he has to run his home and family on the same sort of methodical lines as he runs his office. Always trying to keep the two separate so that his boss never finds out about his lack of control and importance at home.

Well, that is Peter's story. But as TV producer Shaun O'Riordan says, 'Stories in themselves are not funny enough. You need to exploit them with a twist to make them funny.' And that is what the next chapter is about. But, you might start to give a thought to the changes you'd make in Peter's story to give you a greater potential for comedy that would last through a series.

Our concern here is how to show what Peter is like without actually saying it. The knack is to put him in a situation where he has to reveal his characteristics. Not all at one go, obviously, but enough for us to laugh at how he tries to cope with that situation. In the British TV series *Love Thy Neighbour* the writers Vince Powell and Harry Driver made Eddie reveal his hatred of black people by giving him a black next door neighbour. He couldn't ignore the problem. It put him under stress. And that is the best way to show a person's characteristics, put them under stress. Face them with the thing they most fear.

If Peter fears change then we'd have him come home one day and find that Monica had changed the furniture and rearranged the cupboards so that they now house different things. He wouldn't be able to find the things he'd so methodically put in order. At the same time his office is being decorated at work and he is being temporarily switched to another office. These two things combine to play havoc with his normal routined way of life. They put him under stress.

The interesting thing is to see how this will make him react to the people who caused this change. Will he shout at his wife? Will he sulk? Will he try to seek revenge? Will he, as a legal man, search through the reference books to find some obscure law that says a wife cannot make major changes in the home without her husband's consent? Yes, let's explore this avenue a bit further. Supposing the wife retaliates by making sure that she and the three kids actually start to comply to the letter with every ancient law governing the home. That would cause a go-slow in the household that would throw Peter even further off balance.

Now let's put him in another predicament, one of divided loyalties. We'll suppose he is handling a divorce case in which the man is someone very much like himself and is, in Peter's opinion, completely in the right. He makes out a very good case for the man and then finds that it's in fact the woman's side he is supposed to be handling.

Now he finds himself having to make out a good convincing case against someone with his own beliefs, traits and habits. And to further complicate things, this is the one case where Monica has come to court because she is showing some tourist friends the way English law works. Peter spots Monica in the audience and has to suffer the embarrassment of her hearing him expound all her own arguments against himself. And, in order to impress the client and his boss, he has to do it in a very forthright and damning manner. I'm sure you can see how a situation like this would lay Peter's own characteristics wide open for the viewers.

But the important thing to establish that comedy, would be the earlier scene in which Monica had argued those very points with Peter about himself. And we laugh at him actually finding himself quoting her very words in court.

There are certain ways of addressing people or prefacing a line that shows the speaker's attitude to that person. Simple things like if you call someone John it shows you are on friendly terms. If you call them Mr Smith it shows either respect or a distance between you. But if you formerly called him John and now address him as Mr Smith it means that you are deliberately using his surname as a sign of disrespect because you have probably had an argument with him and want to put a barrier between you.

I could say timidly, 'May I tell you something . . .?' Or more belligerently 'Let me tell you this . . .' If I was old fashioned I'd say, 'You kids get away with murder today . . .' But if I was more modern and considerate I'd say, 'You kids are very fortunate in being able to do these things we could never get away with in my day.' If I admired a particular fellow I'd say, 'Old Smith worked hard to make that money.' But if I were jealous of him I'd probably say, 'Old Smith's been very lucky making all that money.' In the way I put that I am really telling the audience more about myself than I am about old Smith.

If some gadget breaks down in the house I might say, 'I must fix that' or alternatively I could say, 'I must fix that sometime.' By merely adding the word 'sometime' I am showing that I am lazy and don't really intend doing it. If I liked the way my neighbour had tended his garden I could tell him, 'You've done a good job there.' Or if I were the gushing type I'd say, 'What a great job you've done with those roses. Oh, you're so clever.' Or if I was angling for his help I'd say, 'I wish I could get my garden like that. I suppose I'll never get to be as good at it as you are. I just don't know where to start.' All these lines tell us something about the character that says them.

I have personally found that several men I know changed when they became taxi drivers. Their constant fight to get through busy traffic in order to earn their living, spilled over into their private lives and made them more aggressive than they'd previously been.

You don't have to be a trained psychologist to see what makes people change their normal behaviour pattern. All you have to do is 'observe'. Observe how a normally placid man will push and shove like a wild animal to squeeze a place for himself in a crowded train. Observe how edgy people become when you invade what they consider to be their territorial space. For instance, next time you're in a cafeteria or diner and have to share a table with a complete stranger, let your plate or cup or saucer overlap into their half of the table and then watch their reaction. It will, most times, make them nervous or even quite hostile.

Even a simple thing like giving up smoking can alter a person's character drastically. Where they were formerly quiet and sedate they suddenly become edgy, intolerant and impatient. They may perhaps give up their addiction to tobacco only to replace it with something else. Perhaps sucking lollipops or chewing gum or even taking up a handicraft of some sort to keep their hands busy. It could even be knitting.

But whatever you choose as a replacement addiction it would — and must for comic purposes — be something we'd be surprised to see that person doing. A butch guy taking up knitting would be a typical example. And you could get a great deal of fun out of him trying to hide the fact that he knits so that he won't be ridiculed.

I think I have given you enough guidance to enable you to find your own characters. Now try describing in detail people you know well. Your description should build up a clear mental picture. Think up circumstances for those characters that would make them funny. You'll be putting them in a situation that is so opposite to those they normally enjoy, that their reactions to it will result in comedy.

7 / Situation Comedy II: Storylines

When you have worked out an idea for a situation comedy series, you should try to put the format down on paper. A format is the basic concept of the series. It tells who the characters are, what their relationship is, and what setting you plan to put them in.

Here is an example of what a format should look like:

Format of: 'IT'S A SMALL WORLD' by Phil White.

Basic Idea:

This is a thirty-minute situation comedy series that features the romance and courtship of an odd couple. Odd because he is only five foot three and she is five foot nine in her stockinged feet. Their common link is an inferiority complex about their own respective heights.

He, Bobby Greenwood, is an Australian radio and TV comedy writer who has come to London to visit a girl he corresponded with as a penfriend up till five years ago. She, Shirley Swales, is now happily married to laboratory assistant Edward Swales, but she has a single sister, Pauline, that has no current boyfriend and who, she thinks, ought to get married.

So Bobby is invited to stay over as a guest of Ed and Shirley Swales with the sly intention of their matchmaking him with tall, shy, dumpy Pauline. It comes as a surprise when they find that Bobby is so short. He never mentioned it in any of his letters.

The Swales expect the pairing of Pauline and Bobby to be a disaster at first sight. But it turns out to be just the opposite. The two soon realise they share opposite ends of the same problem and form an affinity that may eventually lead to marriage.

But till it does, Shirley and Ed are lumbered with their houseguest who has decided to stay and work in England to be near his new found love.

The regular cast consists of just the four characters:

> *Bobby:* Thirty-four-year-old Australian comedy writer who has taken a year's sabbatical to write a comic novel. Part of the reason for his trip to England is to gather background material for the novel. The advance from his Australian publisher provides the money he is able to live on.
>
> Probably the simplest way to describe the appearance of Bobby is to call him an Aussie version of Woody Allen. And he shares a similar sense of humour to Woody, too. It's mostly self-deprecating.
>
> The embarrassment he feels because of his diminutive stature is manifested by his talking too much. And making jokes at times when it would be wiser to stay silent. He knows this fault and tries to control it.
>
> It's best controlled when he is with people with whom he feels comfortable. Then he can relax and be his real sweet, warm hearted, vulnerable self.
>
> After their first meeting Bobby is most relaxed with:
>
> *Pauline:* Twenty-nine years old, librarian. Fairly well educated. Tends, when embarrassed or nervous, to talk about trivia she has read in encyclopaedias or reference books at the library. Soon finds a kindred spirit in Bobby and is relaxed when they are alone. She is a likeable person, but sometimes

we get annoyed at her when she is too lacking in confidence. For instance, if she were applying for a new job she would think up dozens of reasons they could turn her down.

Physically, she is a bit overweight and reminds one of a younger version of Joan Sims.

Pauline is not at all like her slightly elder sister:

Shirley: Thirty-one years old, part time secretary and housewife. Been married three years and still madly in love with her husband. Though keen at first to have Bobby as a guest for one week, she is angry that Ed (the pushover), has agreed to let him stay 'as long as he likes'.

It means extra work for her cleaning his room, doing his laundry and cooking special food because he is a vegetarian and has peculiar tastes. His talking too much annoys her and she is quite sarcastic to him.

But she would also like him out of the way so that she and Ed could be alone again. The room Bobby has is the one Shirley had set aside as a future nursery. She would dearly love to have a child. But everytime she brings up the subject, a decision on it is delayed by:

Edward: Also thirty-one years old. Known as Ed to one and all. A laboratory assistant with high hopes of promotion when he finishes the long term project he is working on.

Ed is very much in love with his wife and usually gives way in any argument just to have a peaceful life. He quite likes Bobby who helps him with the writing of some lab. reports he is preparing for a medical journal.

From the beginning Ed has thought that getting Pauline married off was a good idea. He gets annoyed at her constant interruptions when he is trying to watch his favourite TV shows, always pointing out some uninteresting trivial fact about something on the screen.

Both Ed and Shirley are of normal height and build and quite good looking.

Sets: The main set used in all the episodes is the living room of the Swales' flat . . . with the kitchen/dining room that leads off it. And the small nursery-turned-bedroom that Bobby occupies in the flat will be used frequently too.

Plot Ideas: 1. *Eating Out.* Shirley gets tired of preparing special food for Bobby, so Ed suggests they go out to a restaurant and let someone else do the cooking for a change. They invite Pauline along to make up the foursome.

Though Pauline and Bobby are comfortable with each other despite their height difference, they are very conscious of it when strangers are around. In a restaurant, for instance.

The tall cloakroom attendant is, by sheer coincidence, an old school chum of Pauline's. The two girls were rivals for boyfriends back in the old days, and Pauline is ashamed to be seen with little Bobby as her escort. So she pretends to be Ed's partner.

On his way to the table Bobby senses that most of the other people around are much taller than he is. At the next table are three giant basketball players celebrating a victory. But Bobby's faith in himself is restored when the waiter turns out to be even shorter than he is and has no sense of inferiority at all. He is, in fact, quite arrogant and bossy.

After a while it dawns on Bobby that Pauline is trying to impress the cloakroom girl and he plays along with it. There are comic complications when the girl sees Ed kissing Shirley at the table while Pauline has gone off to the Powder Room.

At the end of the meal Bobby walks on tiptoe to make himself look taller as they collect their hats and coats.

The short waiter chases after them to return a cigarette lighter Pauline had left at the table. The cloakroom girl introduces the waiter to Pauline as her husband. Bobby happily drops down to his normal height again as he proudly walks arm in arm with Pauline out of the restaurant.

2. *The Inside Story.* Bobby announces that he has decided to write a domestic situation comedy show that he will base on Ed and Shirley. He says he sees them as a typical happily married couple that the viewers will be able to identify with.

Both Ed and Shirley are solicited for stories of events during their three years of marriage so that he can use the best for his first episode. They quite like the idea of being model characters.

Bobby discusses the script with Pauline and together they add a few twists to make it funnier. But they are quite surprised when Ed and Shirley are shown the script and hate it. They feel their weaknesses have been accentuated rather than their

124

strengths. In their eyes the characters they have been portrayed as make them look foolish.

They become tight-lipped and refuse to say anything more than is absolutely necessary when Bobby is within earshot.

Bobby sees that he is in danger of being thrown out and gives his script an unexpected twist in the plot that makes them heroes after all.

3. *Two Beds are better than one.* Bobby's cousin from Australia is on a business trip to London and finds his hotel is overbooked. So Ed and Shirley are asked if Mike (the cousin) can share Bobby's room for a couple of days. He will sleep on the floor in a sleeping bag. They reluctantly agree.

Mike turns out to be a real smoothie. Tall, good looking, with a way of chatting up women with believable flattery. He makes a play for Shirley and when she rejects him he turns his attention to Pauline.

Pauline responds, flattered. This causes jealousy between him and Bobby and ends with Bobby throwing his cousin out of the flat.

4. *Bobby shows his appreciation.* Bobby pleases Shirley by saying he is returning to his native Australia next week. At the travel agent's where he has gone to book his flight, he meets a fellow Australian working over here as a freelance decorator. The poor fellow is having a hard time making a living and Bobby decides to help by commissioning him to redecorate Ed and Shirley's lounge. He figures it'll be a nice surprise for them and be his way of saying thank you for all their hospitality.

With the aid of Pauline, he contrives to get Ed and Shirley out of the flat by paying for all four of them to go to a show and a meal after it. During that time, the painter, with Bobby's keys, enters the flat and paints away happily without any interruption.

When they return home they find the man has painted nudes and abstracts on the walls and the colour schemes are pseudo-modern and not at all to Shirley's taste. She gets hysterical.

Bobby hires a proper house painter to repair the damage and do a proper job. But the money he spends on that means he can no longer afford his ticket to Australia. So, once again, Shirley is stuck with him. And Pauline is happy he is staying.

* * *

That is the way a format is laid out. But this particular one didn't sell because the writer gave the impression that the stories would be about the relationship between the tall woman and the short man. Only the first plot idea used that as its basis. The other three stories had nothing to do with the differences in their heights, or even focused on their strange romance and courtship at all.

It is a common fault among new writers that they pick on ideas which they cannot sustain. They become what's known as 'one joke ideas' which quickly exhaust themselves and become repetitious.

Many successful series have developed into something other than what was originally envisioned. The old Dick Van Dyke series is a perfect example of this. The basic concept on which it was sold was that a comedy writer gets the ideas for his sketches and routines from actual experiences in his own life. This worked well for the first series and then it gradually became an ordinary domestic comedy series with the scriptwriter gimmick being quite incidental and sometimes not even mentioned at all.

The Thames Television series *Shelley,* starring Hywel Bennett as an educated layabout who supported his wife and kid on dole money rather than work in a capitalist society, changed as it went along. The writer felt he had exploited all the comedy he could get out of Shelley's married status, so he altered the next series to have him living on his own.

Rhoda, the American comedy series about a Jewish girl living alone in New York, but always under the subtle influence of her worried mother, was beautifully written. But after a while the producers felt it needed a radical change, so they got her married.

That worked well for a couple of series, but then they felt that being married made her too protected. It lessened the amount of situations she could get involved in where she'd be vulnerable enough for the viewers to worry about her wellbeing and safety. So they got her divorced and wrote out the husband.

These changes are simple to make and often quite necessary to keep a long running series seem fresh. But in order to sell it the writer has to establish he can come up with enough stories to maintain his characters consistently in the first series.

Sometimes writers will run dry on ideas when their series has been running a long time. That's when the producer will throw it open to any experienced writer that can come up with good

126

enough storylines that fit the characters and setting already established.

If I were asked to submit a story line for such a popular series as *Steptoe and Son (Sandford and Son* is the American version), it would need be no longer than this:

Harold and Albert Steptoe are courting two women who are daughter and mother respectively. They set it up to go out on a double date. Meanwhile, on his totting rounds Harold picks up some throw-out misfit dresses from a local gown manufacturers. Both men, unbeknown to each other, steal one of the dresses to give as a present to their lady-loves. They lie about the exclusivity of the dress design and how expensive it was to buy. On the date both women turn up wearing the same dress and nearly kill Harold and Albert.

That's all that's needed for the storyline. Assuming the producer liked it he would ask me to work out the plot and that would mean going into much greater detail. I'd be expected to show how they meet these women. How they court them. How each, at a loss for a present to give the girls, hits separately on the idea of giving them one of the dresses. How both Harold and then Albert deliberately miscount the number of dresses to try and hide the fact that they've stolen one. How the girls are persuaded to believe that the dresses are Paris models and that their boyfriends are both wealthy playboys. Then I'd have to explain the set up for the double date for a meal at a fancy restaurant where the women find that not only are they wearing the same dress, but so is the hatcheck girl who says she got it for nothing as a throw-out from that same gown manufacturer. The mother and daughter throw things at the father and son and walk out in disgust, ending the romance. And I'd show that it ends with Albert more concerned about Harold's stupidity in being conned into buying throw-out dresses when he could have got them for nothing, than he is about losing his gold-digger lady-love.

That basically is the difference between a storyline and a plot. But now that we have touched on this particular plot, let's explore it a little and see how much fun we could get out of it. We already know the two main characters and their relationship to each other so we use that to get their reaction to the situation. We would first establish that, because of their lack of common interests, Harold and Albert are lonely men. Without telling each other, they both apply by letter to a marriage bureau and get dates to meet their new ladyfriends at times just quarter of an hour apart at the same place on the same day. They could all meet there and from the embarrassment of father and son could come lots of laughs.

But on reflection, it would probably be funnier still if we only knew that Harold had arranged a date through the marriage bureau. He'd dress up in his Sunday best and lie to his father about where he was going. And there, at the appointed place for the meeting would be the older woman, who, like her daughter, answers to the name of Ms Bosworth. Harold can't believe that the date they've chosen for him could be that old and she in turn can't believe in her luck in getting such a young man. Then the father turns up in his Sunday best and we realise that he too had applied to a marriage bureau for a date. I think this approach is funnier and probably more in line with the way Galton and Simpson would have written it.

With the two couples it appears to be love at first sight. The men are rather ashamed of being rag and bone merchants and decide to call themselves Antique Dealers. We could have some fun with the dialogue when they talk about how they pick up old items here and there and sell them again for five or six times the price they paid. They are, of course, truthfully talking about their junk but the girls believe they're referring to valuable antiques. And since we, the audience, know something the girls don't know, it is funny. Without needing to establish it in the dialogue we can, by merely having the women look at each other at the appropriate moment, convey the impression that they are aiming to marry rich men. And that they are convinced that the Steptoes are rich.

They arrange another date for later in the week. Meanwhile Harold goes on his rounds with love shining out of his eyes. He's off his food and his mind is only half on his job. The manager of the gown manufacturers tells one of his staff to give the reject dresses away to the rag and bone man. But the smart fellow *sells* them to Harold instead of giving them to him. Harold beats the price down and thinks he's been clever to get them cheap.

Again, on reflection, that scene would be funnier if the man fully intends giving the dresses to Harold for nothing, but Harold doesn't understand this and quotes the top price he's willing to pay. The man tries to explain and Harold, thinking himself to be a smart businessman, is actually cheating himself. The audience will laugh because they know and Harold doesn't.

On the second date the two women give the men small gifts. One gets a tieclip with his initials and the other gets cufflinks with his initials. The men are embarrassed because they haven't been thoughtful enough to bring gifts, but promise to later.

128

So now we've got a reason for each to want to give their female partner one of the dresses. But neither man tells the other and both try to hide that they've taken one by deliberately counting them up as though they were all there. This can also become a very funny scene.

So too can the scene where each presents the dress to his lady and passes it off as a Paris exclusive. Or perhaps it would be better if we did the same as we did at the start, and only have Albert present the dress to his lady and not know what Harold has chosen for the daughter. That would be shown at the end on the final date when both of them turn up wearing the same dress. That is when we realise that Harold has stolen one of the dresses too. They explain that Balmain made just two of these dresses so that the scene can continue with the women more or less appeased until they go to the cloakroom and see the hatcheck girl wearing the same dress. And then a tarty type enters the restaurant on the arm of the man who sold the dresses to Harold in the first place. She too is wearing one of those same dresses. The situation explodes as the girls realise their dates are not rich after all, and so they tear off the tieclip and cufflinks and angrily walk out. And we end, as shown earlier, with Albert shouting at Harold for paying for the dresses he could have got for nothing. And since this shouting takes place at the most exclusive of London's restaurants with Albert lapsing back into his normal foul-mouthed Cockney expressions, it must be funny by contrast to the rather distinguished clientele. We'll have had a fair quota of laughs in the show and the audience will be happy that the Steptoes have been saved from the clutches of the two female bloodsuckers. That is the plot. And you've seen me working it out here for you the way a professional writer would go about it.

New writers always wonder how you ring the changes in the plots when your regular cast is say, only four characters and you are confined to using just the three regular sets built for the series. The answer is simple and quite obvious when you think about it. What you have to do is find a reason to make those regular few characters behave differently by bringing in an outsider who is alien to their normal way of life. Or, if not a person, then a situation that will disturb their normal habits or routine.

Do you remember the Steptoe episode where Harold brought home a French girl he had fallen in love with and then found out that his father had been sewing his wild oats in France during the war and the girl is his own sister? The mere fact that this pretty and sweet young French girl was in the hovel they call their home, changed their normal way of life while she was there with them. They were both trying to impress her. Steptoe senior dropped his dirty habits and Harold left off insulting his father. The show's writers had given them a legitimate reason to be other than their normal selves and this contrast to the way we knew them was funny.

We could make it more obvious by having had Harold corresponding with a pen pal in Sweden and then have her come over. The rather permissive society that she comes from would be completely alien to the narrow-minded way Steptoe senior likes to keep things. And she would even embarrass the would-be lecherous Harold by too obviously trying to seduce him in front of his father. I see an episode such as this being easy to set up and equally easy to score laughs from. And all we've had to do is bring in one extra character.

If we wanted to take the same theme to a greater extreme, his pen pal would be a Japanese lady. To make her feel more at home Harold would decorate the place in Geisha style. His father fought the Japanese in the war and hates them. So when the girl arrives he keeps making jibes about his war wounds and how he suffered so that the Japanese nation could become so prosperous and undercut our car prices. The laughs would come from the contrast in the Japanese style decor to the squalid style they're used to and then from Harold's fruitless efforts to silence his father's cutting remarks. And perhaps even giving him a Hari-Kari knife and hoping he'll take the hint.

Let's find another reason to change the decor so that we can get laughs out of the resulting contrast. Harold has joined the local Conservative Party because he feels that he ought to mix with what he considers to be a higher class of people. At the party meeting he teams up with another Conservative who is the son of a lord and Harold brings the chap home to try and impress his own father. The visitor turns out to have a penchant for interior decorating and immediately offers to turn the Steptoes' home into something much more modern. Steptoe senior refuses and Harold, to assert his independence, tells his new friend that it's all right to go ahead and do his half of the house. The result will be that half of the main room is done in a sort of Picasso style which sharply contrasts with the other half which stays as it was. And probably the tag to this one would be Harold receiving an unexpected bill for the job which he thought was being done on a friendly basis for nothing. It fits in with the regular theme of the series that every time Harold defies his father he winds up being caught by an outsider.

*   *   *

Let's go back to the beginning and I'll work through a format and storylines for a new situation comedy. The first thing to decide on are the lead characters and their relationship to each other. Who they are. What they are. And where they are.

The easiest thing to go for is the relationship between a man and woman because both sexes in the audience can identify with that. But there are an enormous number of husband and wife situation comedies so I'd like to avoid that. British comedian/scriptwriter Eric Sykes got his man/woman relationship by writing comedienne Hattie Jacques in as his twin sister. That way they were able to live together without any emotional entanglement. But I would like to *have* emotional entanglement without necessarily setting the show in a house or an apartment for the usual run of domestic comedy.

Let's make it an office with the man as the boss and the woman as his quite attractive secretary who loves him and is frustrated because he never even considers her as anything but an employee. To him she's just part of the furniture.

His function is to run his business as efficiently as possible. Hers is to be a good secretary, but also to try and get him to be attracted to her as a woman. And her ultimate goal is to ensnare him into marriage. Both of them are, of course, single. I see her as about twenty-eight and him as about thirty-four. Let's give them names so it's easier to refer to them. I'll call her Tessa and him Daniel.

We will need to decide what business he has and it ought to be something that won't require too much research on my part. I think I'll try making him an insurance broker because I have several uncles and cousins in insurance that I could ring up for advice if needed.

We now have our two leading characters, the business they are in, and their relationship to each other. The generic set (that's the one used over and over throughout the series) is their office suite. Daniel has the inner office and Tessa has the outer one.

As I see it, Tessa will be motivating most of the plots and therefore I need to have the audience know what's going on in her scheming mind. To do this I will have to use another character that Tessa can confide in. In fact I'll borrow the same gimmick used for this on the *Rhoda* series and make it Tessa's sister. So each episode starts with Tessa and her sister, Liz, talking on the phone to each other before their respective bosses arrive at the office.

Liz should have an identity of her own, rather than just being Tessa's sister. If you remember, Rhoda's sister, Brenda, always talked about her weight problem and her inferiority complex. Maybe Liz could be studying something in evening classes that she tries to apply to her daily life. It could be yoga, for instance. My wife is a yoga teacher so I know a bit about the subject. I could also make Liz an ardent Women's Libber so that would cut out any thoughts of her wanting to get married. It also makes her try to get Tessa to give up being (as she sees it) Daniel's slave.

Another character, to be used when necessary, is Henry. He's an author who writes novels. Tessa works for him some evenings typing out his manuscripts. That supplements the rather poor wages that she gets from Daniel. Without these extra earnings Tessa would have had to leave Daniel and get a better paying job. She's certainly efficient enough for better pay, but Daniel's still building up his business and can't yet afford to pay her higher wages. And anyway, Tessa would work for him for even less because she loves the guy.

Henry appreciates Tessa's efficiency. She not only types fast, but she also corrects his spelling and grammar where necessary. He offers her a full time job working for him at a third more than Daniel pays her. So, as we open the first episode of the series, we find Tessa reading the note from Henry making this generous offer. I say 'reading' rather than just telling Liz about it, because it needs to be in writing so that Daniel can later find it. That forms part of the plot.

In that opening phone conversation Liz tries to talk Tessa into accepting Henry's offer, but Tessa makes it clear she'd never consider leaving Daniel unless he made it patently obvious he wasn't going to return her love. While she has even the faintest hope of marrying Daniel she'll stay on as his secretary.

What I must do now is construct a situation where Daniel, knowing Tessa is short of money, finds the note from Henry and believes she'll accept the offer. He doesn't realise that Tessa loves him and can't see any reason why she would not accept the offer. So, in order not to be left without a secretary, Daniel phones an employment agency to get himself a replacement.

If you're thinking along the same lines as I am you will arrange in the script for Tessa to answer the call from the employment agency saying they haven't a girl available at the moment, but will have one by the end of the week. And Tessa's reaction is one of shock. She doesn't know that Daniel has seen the note from Henry. All she knows is that he is trying to get a new secretary to replace her. She is hurt that Daniel hasn't even mentioned it to her and thinks he is doing it behind her back. And when Daniel found the note he too was hurt that Tessa hadn't told him she was going to leave and was negotiating for the new job behind *his* back.

There we have set the plot. All we need is to have them both act naturally in what they think is the situation and we should be able to get comedy from it. Tessa thinks she has till the end of the week to change Daniel's mind about getting rid of her. So she will be over-attentive to him. Over-efficient in her work. But it will meet with a cold, unresponsive reception from Daniel because he is still annoyed that she hasn't been honest enough to tell him she's leaving. He just assumes she's getting the filing and correspondence right up to date to soften the blow when she announces she's quitting to work for Henry.

Tessa is starting to think that Daniel is inhuman. She's putting in all this extra effort for him without as much as a thank you. Tessa begins to have doubts about whether Daniel is really the nice kind of guy she thought he was. Because, as far as she is concerned, he is still going ahead with bringing in a new secretary to replace her.

At this stage I could have Henry disappointed that his offer has been turned down. Firstly because he appreciated Tessa as a good secretary, and secondly because he fancies her as a woman. So he comes to the office to talk to Daniel about sharing her on a fifty-fifty basis. But Tessa pre-empts this by saying she will now agree to work for Henry full time. It's a decision she's made on the advice of her sister, Liz. But it's obvious that Tessa still thinks the world of Daniel and says she'll stay on long enough to train a new secretary, as she knows that Daniel has requested one from the agency. Both Tessa and Daniel still feel the other has let them down. I could end it here with a confrontation scene between them in which they realise they've both jumped to conclusions and there's been a silly mistake.

But I'm opting for bringing in the new secretary for Tessa to train so that she can point out to her all of Daniel's idiosyncrasies and set ways which could be a trifle annoying to the new girl, but which are endearing to Tessa who loves him. This gives the audience a chance to learn more about Daniel in a simple legitimate way.

Alternatively, I could change the plot and have Tessa find out that Daniel discovered the note and is hiring a new secretary because he thought she was leaving and that things have gone too far for him to back out now. If that were the case, Tessa's scheming mind would immediately start working on a way to have him get rid of the new girl. And the way to do that might be to have her sister, Liz, take a day off from her own job and come in as the very inept new girl. She'd deliberately louse up so many things that Daniel would end up begging Tessa to stay on. And Tessa would make a big show of her loyalty in doing so.

Either of these situations could work. If Daniel already knew Liz then we'd give her a blonde wig, Cockney accent and way-out clothes so she would not be recognised. And as we'll have established her norm at the start of the show, her playing this part out of character must be funny.

Well, that takes care of the main plot. Here's what I think may be a good thing to go for for the sub-plot, because up till now we have not used the fact that he's an insurance broker and not done much with Liz's leanings to Women's Lib.

Two of Daniel's clients who have their cars insured through him have an accident. Their cars crash into each other without it really being clear whose fault it is. It's one of those cases where both drivers were partly in the wrong but each blames the other because neither wants to lose his treasured no-claims bonus. Both put in their own version of how the crash occurred and how it was the other driver's fault. The important thing is that one of the drivers is a man and the other a woman. Daniel is inclined to see more merit in the man's version . . . but Tessa, spurred on by Liz's belief that women should stick together, re-writes the woman's version on the claims form in order to strengthen it.

The male driver is a more important client and so Daniel advises him while secretly Tessa advises the woman driver. It could end up with both clients getting so deep into perjury, hiring false witnesses, that each loses their no-claims bonus and Daniel loses their future business.

Obviously it would need more refining and defining than that, but there is the basis of the idea I'd work on to get a good plot out of the characters. It puts Daniel and Tessa in a position of stress and conflict and is the quickest way to show the audience how they relate to each other.

Someone once said that the test of true love between a couple is that they know something really hurtful they can say to the other, but even the height of battle doesn't make them resort to saying it. So, much as Tessa and Daniel may resent each other's actions in the main plot, they never say anything really hurtful. Because both know that if they did, that would be the end of their relationship.

Anyway, right off the top of my head, that is probably the

way I would construct a storyline to fit the characters I've chosen.

It's important that the characters be so different from each other that their dialogue lines are not interchangeable. Henry, the novelist, would be a lecherous type who keeps asking Tessa to act out the love scenes with him so that he can see how best to write them. She fights him off but would gladly have accepted the same suggestion from Daniel, if it ever came. To her frustration, it never does.

* * *

There is no set rule about writing the guaranteed successful situation comedy series. But there are lots of things that help prevent it being a failure. The first is to use characters that you know you can sustain and who are believable, interesting and attractive to watch. Then to make sure that those characters have an identity of their own. It is important to make sure that these people will contrast sufficiently to show up each others traits and attitudes clearly. (Think of the three people Johnny Speight put up against Alf Garnett — his wife, daughter and son-in-law — all completely different from himself in appearance, temperament and attitude.)

The final thing is to concoct or discover a situation that highlights their differences and has conflict and intrigue. If your lead character has only one choice of action and takes it, then your story lacks intrigue. Wherever possible, give him at least two choices of action so that neither he, nor the audience can be sure how it will turn out.

Keep upsetting the apple cart. When it looks as though one problem is solved then you should make it lead to another problem. And another. Two semi-climaxes and one final climax is just about right. For commercial TV it's good to have your lead character in trouble just before the commercial break. Your audience should be hooked to their sets wondering how he/she is going to get out of their problem. It's the *Perils of Pauline* system where every episode ended with poor Pauline tied to the railway tracks or about to be cut in half in a sawmill. The only difference is that you have to have a definite end to each episode and put your railway track or sawmill along the way.

When I started out as a writer there were no schools to teach you how to write comedy. The only way you could learn was by watching what the existing writers were doing. So I stayed in every night glued to my radio or television and took note of everything I saw and heard in a comedy show. After a while I began to realise how many shows were using the same plots and situations without the general public ever realising it. The plots *seemed* different because they were approached by different characters. Here are some samples of storylines of some of the plots I recognised being duplicated by several different series:

1. One of the characters would find a stray dog and bring it home to his flat where pets are not allowed. The head of the household claims to hate dogs, but we see his resistance to canines gradually being weakened till he becomes very much attached to the poor little mutt. He is as sad as the rest of the family when the dog's rightful owner shows up and he has to part with it. With the reward money he buys a little puppy.

2. Mother wants a food mixing machine which her husband refuses to buy for her. He says it's an unnecessary luxury that they can manage without. Then mother reads of a cooking competition where the prize is a food mixer. She is determined to win and during the next two weeks tries hard, experimenting with all the dishes on the family. They hate the exotic dishes and, not wishing to offend mother, they pretend to eat the food but secretly stuff it in their pockets or feed it to the cat who becomes (mysteriously) ill. But because they are not eating the food, the family are starving. So, in the end out of self defence, the whole family club together to buy mother her food mixing machine.

3. One of the characters has witnessed a bank robbery and has been quoted in the newspaper as having seen the whole thing and being able to give a clear description of the gunman who shot the bank teller. He is very proud at having his name and picture in all the papers. But then the gunman, arrested on his evidence, escapes. So the pride quickly turns to fear. And everyone who comes to the house is suspected of being the killer in disguise come to bump off the witness. The dustman, the new milkman, the gas meter man . . . they're all treated as unwanted intruders by the now terrified witness. In the end he knocks out a man who manages to get in and then finds this was the chap from the bank bringing him a reward for helping to catch the gunman in the first place.

4. Father admonishes his son for telling a small fib and teaches him that he should always be honest. Then the kid catches his father out in an instance when they have guests over and is using tact instead of saying what the kid knows

they really think. The child blurts out the truth and the guests leave in a huff. And then the show ends with the kid admonishing his father for not being honest.

5. A married couple get drawn into an argument that another married couple are having. The wife takes sides with the other wife and the husband takes sides with her husband. The second couple kiss and make up while the couple who were drawn into it are still left arguing amongst themselves.

6. A married couple have a single and quite eligible young male friend that they think ought to get married and settle down. They also know of a girl who is looking for a husband. They tell both their friends about the other and both insist they would not feel right about being thrown together. Instead they would like to meet at a party where, if they didn't like each other, they could avoid embarrassment and just mix with the others at the party. So the party is arranged at the house of yet another couple. Because the room is crowded, when the single boy and girl are pointed out to each other they think they are being pointed to the handsome and beautiful host and hostess. They like what they see. So the single boy makes a play for the hostess and the girl does the same with the host. They almost break up the marriage of the host and hostess who accuse each other of infidelity. And the couple who started the whole thing in the first place decide not to meddle with other people's lives in future.

7. A husband is stopped by a newspaper reporter conducting a survey and asked, 'Do you think that it's right that a woman's place is in the kitchen and tending to the kids and a man's place is at work earning money to keep the family?' He is quoted in the newspaper as saying he wholeheartedly agrees with that. He is happy about having his name in the paper until his wife rolls it up round a rolling pin and hits him over the head with it. She doesn't agree and decides to show him how wrong he is by acting the dumb and deferential wife whose brain is fit for nothing but cooking, washing, sewing, ironing and tending the children's needs.

8. The husband reads somewhere that wives tend to get bored and develop a roving eye if they haven't anything else interesting to do. So he encourages his wife to take up a hobby. She decides on painting. Everything is fine while she is painting inanimate objects, but when she graduates to

painting live models, and when they're male and handsome . . . jealousy sets in and the plot thickens or at least gets lumpy.

9. The newlyweds both secretly take part time jobs in order to be able to afford a really good first anniversary present for each other. But since neither knows where the other disappears to in the evening they begin to suspect infidelity. So that the plot doesn't fizzle out too quickly, the wife tells her husband she is visiting her mother and the husband claims to be visiting a sick workmate in hospital. He phones her mother and finds she's been lying and later she goes along to the hospital and finds the workmate was discharged weeks ago. They think that their spouse is playing around and decide that what's good for the goose is good for the gander. So each actually tries to do what the other one suspects them of, but since they really love each other they can't go through with it. They break down, confess and the plot goes on happily ever after.

10. The husband has been promoted at work and is required to attend a society ball with his wife. He promises to buy her an exclusive dress that she has seen in the window of a Bond Street shop. But when he finds out the exorbitant price he realises that it's ridiculous to lay out all that money so she can wear the dress for this one occasion only. So, unbeknown to her, he hires a little dressmaker to make a copy of it. Meanwhile, the wife has found out the price of the dress and thinks her husband is absolutely marvellous in spending all that money on her. In gratitude she treats him like a king and waits on him hand and foot. And then, when she gets to the ball, she finds that the original dress is being worn by the wife of her husband's boss. And to cap it all there are several other women there wearing the same copy of that exclusive dress made by the same crooked little dressmaker.

They are just a few that I remember seeing various permutations on in the early days when I started making notes on comedy writing. And I soon learnt that if you take any one of those storylines and put it through the computer, as done by different characters from any existing or defunct situation comedy show, they will come out different. The point being that the different characters would react to those situations in their own way.

While I'm making lists, here are some outlines of recent American TV series seen in Britain, with their preview descriptions from the magazine *TV Guide*.

1. **Mork and Mindy** The guy in the red jammies (pyjamas to us British) with the Tupperware on his head is dressed that way because he has recently saucered in from the Planet Ork. He is Mork (Robin Williams) and he has been assigned to act as an advance scout for other Orkians who may want to migrate to Earth. When he lands in Boulder, Colorado, he is befriended by a pretty earthling named Mindy (Pam Damber). She tries to explain the strange folkways of the human race, such as love, old age and junk food — not to mention a procession of bewildered dates, none of whom can understand why this spacey character is always hanging around Mindy's apartment. They don't know what she knows — that Mork hails from another planet and is not merely a *Let's Make a Deal* (game show) contestant who got on the wrong line. Mork was first seen in a *Happy Days* episode, and this series is out of the same situation comedy stable.

2. **Taxi** 'Why is everybody here just a little bit angry?' asks a newly hired cab driver. The answer is obvious; these are New York cabbies, which means they have exhaust fumes coming out of their mouths as well as their tailpipes. At the Sunshine Cab Company everybody is a loser of some kind. One driver is a prize fighter who seldom wins a bout. Another is an actor who can't land any roles. The mechanic speaks a strange language nobody can understand. The dispatcher is a bossy little twerp. Everybody gets on everybody else's nerves. Still, when somebody needs help, they all rally round the motor flag and pull together to bring each episode to a reasonably happy ending.

3. **The Associates** Two keen-minded, young law-school graduates, Leslie Dunn (Alley Mills) and Tucker Kerwin (Martin Short), accept an offer to join Bass and Marshall, a New York law firm. This is their first mistake. Bass and Marshall practise Murphy's Law (if anything can go wrong in this office it will) and Rangnekar's Law (if you can avoid a decision, don't delay). Senior partner Emerson Marshall (Wilfrid Hyde White) is an absent-minded babbler; Eliot Streeter (Joe Ragalbutt) is a self-seeking simp; Sara James (Shelley Smith) is a calculating vamp; and office boy Johnny

Danks (Tim Thomerson) is a swaggering stud. This vehicle — fuelled, let us pray, by laughing gas — is brought to you by the makers of *Taxi*.

4. **Nobody's Perfect** Mrs Troy's jewels are missing from her suite in a posh San Francisco hotel, and in their place is a toy rubber mouse. Must be the work of a thief with a sense of humour — either that or a rubber cat burglar. But not to worry; Inspector Roger Hart (Ron Moody) of Scotland Yard is on the scene. A devilishly suave, debonair chap with just one tiny flaw — he is incapable of moving a muscle without knocking over a lamp, smashing the water cooler and generally wreaking havoc. Hart is in San Francisco on an exchange programme between the San Francisco Police Department and Scotland Yard, which clearly got the better of the deal. But in a triumph of mind over motor impairment, Hart always gets his crook — in this case the notorious Ocelot, a cat burglar indeed. Hart is assisted by Det. Jennifer Dempsy (Cassie Yates) and they both report to Lt. Vince de Gennaro (Michael Durrell), who can usually be found, of course, on the verge of a Hart attack.

5. **Benson** Benson (Robert Guillaume), who played the butler in *Soap,* was not only the sanest one on that show, but the smartest. He has spun himself off from the looney Tate family into a series of his own. Now he's a butler in a Governor's mansion, but the family is as witty as ever. He gets his usual cordial welcome: 'The dogs tried to attack me, the gardener tried to drown me, the security men frisked me, and now I get a storm trooper after my shoes!' The storm trooper is Gretchen Kraus (Inga Swenson), the housekeeper, who makes Lizzie Borden look like Rebecca of Sunnybrook Farm. Governor Gatling (James Noble) is a well-meaning but addlepated sort whose sinking ship of state is kept afloat only by Benson's intervention. Caroline McWilliams, as the Governor's secretary, and Missy Gold as his daughter, are on hand to help Benson steer the Guv from politics to sanity — a long journey.

6. **Ladies' Man** Alan Thackeray (Lawrence Pressman) has been hired as the token male on *Woman's Life,* a magazine whose staff is thoroughly female. There's Susan (Allison Argo), who's level headed; Gretchen (Simone Griffeth), who's into feminism; and Andrea (Betty Kennedy) who's man crazy.

The editor, Elaine Holstein (Louise Sorel), greets Alan's arrival like a visitation of psoriasis. 'I have two unassigned articles for this issue,' she tells him. 'One of them is "Seventeen Ways With Tuna Fish",' she tells him, to which Alan says: 'I'll take the other one.' Holstein: 'I thought you would.' Alan: 'What is it?' Holstein: 'Sexual Harrassment and the Working Woman.'

When not being harassed by Holstein, Alan trades quips with his daughter Amy, 9 (Natasha Ryan), and his neighbour Betty (Karen Morrow), who is always willing to be helpful: 'Call me old fashioned, but I think sexual harassment belongs in the home.'

7. **Love, Sidney** This series is based on a TV-movie *Sidney Shorr,* in which Tony Randall stars as a commercial artist who's gay — and very lonely. His empty life is brightened by the appearance of Laurie Morgan, an aspiring young actress who's sweet, kooky, full of life. Before you can say platonic, she has moved into Sidney's eight-room apartment.

When Laurie falls in love and gets pregnant by a man who turns out to be married, Sidney becomes a surrogate father to the little girl, Patti, whom he loves 'higher than anyone can count'.

You might find it a useful and enlightening exercise to draw up a list of your own favourite situation comedy series and attempt to summarise the idea behind them as succinctly as this.

* * *

In Chapter Six I quoted part of the opening scene of a situation comedy where a husband and wife talk about her hypochondriac brother who is staying with them. After that opening scene has been established, the plot can go off in any direction you like. You will have set the threat. Whatever the job is that Roy is going to do and no matter how bad he is at it, he must make every effort to hold on to it or else he'll find himself homeless. So the writer will obviously select a job that clashes with Roy's worries about his health. It could, for instance, be in a paint factory and Roy believes he is allergic to paint fumes. A lot of people actually are and can't stand being in a newly painted room. Or you could make it some sort of chemical factory that's likely to have more toxic fumes. We're getting into the area of panic comedy. That's to say, the comedian/actor has to go

141

against his natural tendencies in order to cope with the situation he's landed in.

The best example of panic comedy occurs in that now classic film *Some Like It Hot* where Tony Curtis and Jack Lemmon have to disguise themselves as girls because of the situation they've landed in. If you remember the film you'll recall that they were in a garage when some gangsters machine gunned their rival crooks.

Curtis and Lemmon are the only witnesses to the massacre. Throughout the film there's the threat that they too are about to be gunned down to stop them blabbing to the police. The threat is kept alive so that they are 'locked in' to the situation of having to be unrecognisable. They join the band of women musicians and most of the comedy comes from the hazards of having to be someone else (in this case two women) and act against their own tendencies.

What is absolutely essential in these cases is that the threat is real. In *Some Like It Hot* we saw the actual massacre with the blood streaming out on the floor. If we had merely heard about the massacre instead of seeing it, the film would have been a lot weaker. In fact, it just wouldn't have worked for comedy. And also we had to keep seeing the gangsters searching for them with guns to keep the threat alive.

Channel Four have been repeating that ageless American comedy series *Get Smart* with comedian Don Adams as inept Secret Agent Maxwell Smart working with a very pretty female partner known simply as Agent 99. The show, incidentally, was intended to be a send-up of the popular drama series *The Man From U.N.C.L.E.* But it stood up so well on its own most people forgot that.

I mention *Get Smart* because it is a fine example of what I call 'underplayed comedy panic'. For instance, in one episode Maxwell Smart and Agent 99 have won a Kewpie Doll at a fairground and are unaware that it contains lethal drugs. But the dreaded K.A.O.S. agents know and try to snatch the doll and kill Smart and 99 at the same time.

The writer got a hilarious four minute scene out of this by having them go for an innocent fun ride on the fairground's Ghost Train. The K.A.O.S. agents follow and, in the darkness, throw knives and axes which miss our hero and his partner by fractions of an inch. And they enjoy it thinking it's all part of the ride.

They start to realise that something is wrong when their eyebrows are singed by a huge flame shot out of a dragon's mouth. Then, when a hairy hand reaches out and tries to grab

142

the doll, Smart and 99 know they are in danger, and that the narrow misses on their lives were for real. That's when panic sets in.

Getting hastily off the train they try to find their way out through the labyrinth of dark corridors, fighting skeletons, mechanical spiders and painted ogres with blood curdling screams. Each time they think they have found an escape route they come face to face with a K.A.O.S. man and have to double back and find another way.

It was frightening and funny. But only really funny because it *was* frightening. Just as in *Some Like It Hot,* the threat on their lives was clearly established and believable. And the laughs started to build from the moment Maxwell Smart thought those dangerous attempts on his life were just a normal part of the ride. Once again the comedy springs from the fact that we, the viewers, know the true circumstances while the characters on the screen don't. And because the characters were so well written it never, for one moment, seemed contrived.

Rejections so often result from a writer too obviously contriving a comedy situation. He is asking the producer to accept something that he instinctively knows could never happen. Suppose a script called for a man to have taken a prescription to a chemist and when he returned later to collect it, was given someone else's pills or medicine by mistake. This could lead to all manner of comical repercussions. But if the way he got that wrong medicine in the first place is contrived, the script will be rejected.

It's no use saying there were two people named Robinson and he got the other Robinson's sleeping pills by mistake. Chemists are legally obliged to ask for the name and address of the customer before handing over whatever his prescription was for. The plot would have to start further back than that.

A good way to begin it would be with a husband and wife both having different ailments they need to see their doctor about. Neither wants to worry the other and so sneak out to visit the doctor on their own. Neither knows the other has been or that they have been given a prescription they have left with the same chemist. So, when they collect their spouse's medicine by mistake they could believably have told the chemist the same surname and address.

And it is funnier because we can now see them both suffering the reaction to the wrong medicine at the same time in the same set. The contrived coincidence of there happening to be two people with the same surname is no longer there. This plot could easily have fitted into *Steptoe and Son* or almost any situation comedy series in which the two characters live together.

Perhaps you'd like to conjure up in your mind a situation where the husband, because of whatever job you choose for him, needs pep pills to keep awake and his wife, an insomniac, needs sleeping pills to get some rest. Get their pills switched the way we have just discussed and take it from there. Explore how the drowsiness will affect his work and the further lack of sleep will make her act like a zombie. Using your own characters in a setting you're familiar with, you could end up with a really funny script.

8 / Selling Your Work

A recurrent question asked by new writers is how long a situation comedy script should be. In running time it should last about twenty-five and a half minutes for commercial television and about twenty-eight minutes for the B.B.C. For America it would be only twenty-two minutes because they have more commercial and station identification breaks than in Britain.

How long is that in actual script pages? There is no hard and fast answer to that. It depends a lot on how much dialogue there is and how much visual content. A funny car chase where no word is spoken can be described in say, a third of a page and yet last a minute and a half on the screen. But dialogue covering that period of time might take up two full pages.

Not all your characters will talk at the same speed. Jimmy Tarbuck, Ted Rogers and Lennie Bennett will use up twice as many gags in the same time as Max Bygraves, Des O'Connor or Dave Allen. Bob Hope's writers aimed for five big laughs a minute while Jack Benny's were content with two.

The only real effective way to time a script is to read it out aloud to yourself and mime the visual bits as best you can. Ronnie Wolfe who, with his partner Ronnie Chesney, wrote *On the Buses* for five years, says they always went into rehearsal with a thirty page script. They'd expect to cut out two pages at the first script read-through because the cast did not like or appreciate some of the gags. That left a twenty-eight page script as the right length for that series. Each page having an average of ten short speeches.

Reading your script out loud yourself is something you should do anyway. It will often make you realise that you have written lines that are almost impossible to say. Long sentences which do not allow the actor enough pauses to breathe. So when they get to the important punchline their voice is too weak to declaim it as they should.

The second most frequently put question is how important it is to have your script laid out correctly. As any salesman will tell you, the packaging is the first thing that the prospective buyers sees and the more attractive it is, the more chance there is of a sale. We have all heard of the legendary Hollywood film writer who got a million dollars for an idea he had just scribbled on the back of an envelope. But that is something very rare indeed. In fact, there are exceedingly few producers or script editors who will even read a script that is not typewritten.

British TV companies will expect to receive scripts typed out only on the right hand side of the page. That leaves a half page margin on the left for the director to insert his camera shots. It is also used during rehearsals for notes concerning props required, or costumes, or background music or to write in new and replacement dialogue.

Here's a short scene from a situation comedy series starring Bernard Bresslaw and Derek Dene and includes the director's notes on the left. It also shows how you should use capital letters to differentiate directions and dialogue.

BOOM 1C

118. CUT 2G 2″	Sc. 6. INT. THE TENT. DAY.

MCU action back.
M2S Derek & Bernie.

DEREK LAYS HIS PLATE AND CUP ON ORANGE BOX AS BERNIE ENTERS.

BERNIE: Good morning.

DEREK: Oh, it's you again, is it? Didn't you do enough damage yesterday?

BERNIE: I'm sorry you got kicked out of your digs. But I did lend you my Dad's tent, didn't I?

DEREK: Yeah. What's this tent here for anyway?

119. CUT 1G 3″
MS Derek.
BERNIE: The council put it here to watch some valuable equipment.

120. CUT 2G 2″
M2S
DEREK: I don't see any valuable equipment.

BERNIE: No, it was stolen.

121. CUT 3H 3″
MS Bernie.
DEREK: Didn't your Dad get into trouble?

BERNIE: Yeah. He stole it! But they forgot to move the tent so he's been living in it ever since.

122. CUT 1G 3″
MS Derek.

DEREK: Here, your Dad did wash, didn't he?

123. CUT 2G 2″
M2S

BERNIE: Yeah. Why?

147

DEREK: (LOOKING AROUND) What did he use for water?

124. CUT 1G 3''
MS Derek.

BERNIE: The tap.

DEREK: Yes, of course. Silly of me to ask really. (STILL FRANTICALLY LOOKING FOR THE TAP). I mean, it's the obvious thing to do, use the tap . . . (GIVES UP).

125. CUT 2G 3''
MS Bernie pan down to floor.

Where is it?

BERNIE: Under your feet!

CAMERA PANS DOWN TO FLOOR TO SEE THAT DEREK WAS STANDING NEXT TO A HYDRANT. BERNIE LIFTS THE STONE AND PULLS THE PIPE UP. IT'S A PIPE WITH TWO TAPS LEADING OFF IT.

BERNIE: There you are . . . Hot . . . and . . . Cold. All the mod. cons. Even a plug down there for an electric shaver. (HE POINTS DOWN THE HOLE). It's off the mains of the house

126. CUT 1G 2''
M2S

behind us.

DEREK: Ain't that stealing?

BERNIE: Well, Dad had an arrangement with the man who lived there.

DEREK: What sort of an arrangement?

BERNIE: The man didn't know and Dad didn't tell him! But there's a new bloke just moved in so you'd

148

better be careful. He's a copper.
It's a wonder Dad didn't complain
about him lowering the tone of the
neighbourhood!

SWING BOOM 1C

That was part of the 'shooting script' which means it was the final script and the director had added in the shot numbers . . . the camera lens sizes . . . and the type of shot he wanted. MCU meant medium close-up. M2S was medium two shot. MS denoted just a medium shot.

Normally in British comedy scripts the writer does not get involved in the camera work. He just provides the script and the director decides how it is to be best covered by the cameras.

American writers usually suggest the camera angles they want so as to give the director a fuller picture of the way they themselves see their work on the screen. But I've known British directors who get upset when they think the writer is trespassing on their territory.

A careful glance at that script excerpt will show you that the professional writer puts only the dialogue (the spoken word), in small letters. Everything else is in capital letters. Descriptions of action taking place during the speeches are not only in capital letters but are enclosed in brackets so as not to be confused with the dialogue itself.

As I said earlier, packaging is important. First impressions mean a lot. If you want a producer to think your script was written by a professional, it has to be set out the way an experienced writer would do it.

It might sound strange, but scripts have been turned down for being too funny. The writers, desperate to prove they know how to construct funny lines, will overload the script with them. Every character becomes a Bob Hope or Phyllis Diller spouting gags at a machine gun pace.

Think about your own circle of friends, relatives or acquaintances and you are bound to find one that you avoid because they try to be funny all the time and are a bore. They'll pick up on every word you say and make a gag or pun on it. The annoying thing is that they never pay proper attention to the point of your conversation because they are interrupting continually in an attempt to impress you with their wit.

You can't expect television audiences to warm to people like that. And perhaps the one thing that is more essential than anything else is that your viewers like your central characters. This is why many comedians have been failures in situation comedy. They feel awkward about doing lines that don't have a laugh at the end. I've seen them go home at night with a good, well balanced script and come back next morning with a string of gags they've slotted into it for insurance. Gags that destroyed the believability of character and situation.

In a successful situation comedy series my order of priorities as a writer would be keeping the production costs low, using believable situations, making the lead characters someone the audience can identify with and finally making the whole package funny. Not necessarily hilarious. Funny is enough.

Comedy comes under the umbrella heading of Light Entertainment. The purpose of Light Entertainment is to cheer you up. To make you feel a little better than before. This can be achieved by getting the viewers to enjoy nice things happening to people they care for on the screen. In *The Good Life*, written by Esmonde and Larbey they always included at least one scene where the stars Richard Briers and Felicity Kendal kissed, cuddled and said tender things to each other. These scenes weren't particularly funny, but were tremendously effective. As the saying goes, all the world loves a lover. On the screen we saw that Richard and Felicity really cared for each other and it automatically made us care for them. Their joys became ours too.

The format for *It's A Small World* in Chapter Seven gave us the characters of Shirley and Edward Swales who could play that same sort of scene. If I were asked to write an opening sequence to establish their loving relationship it would be along these lines:

> *Interior.   Kitchen.   Day.*
>
> *As we fade up on the scene, Shirley is stirring something in a steaming saucepan on the gas stove.*
>
> *Ed enters, sneaks up behind her and kisses her affectionately on the back of the neck. She reacts startled.*
>
> *Shirley:* Careful! This saucepan's hot!
> *Ed:* So am I. It isn't every day I get to celebrate a third wedding anniversary. Come here.

He pulls her round to face him and kisses her full on the lips.

The kiss lasts about four seconds and starts to get passionate . . . but it's stopped when Shirley pushes him away with her kitchen-gloved hands.

Shirley: (Good natured) Ed, I'm in the middle of cooking. There's a time and place for that kind of thing.
Ed: I entirely agree. *(Looks at his watch)* The time is now twelve thirty. You name the place.
Shirley: (Smiles and sighs) I really don't know what I'm going to do with you.
Ed: Leave that to me. I've got a few good ideas.
Shirley: (Laughing) You're incorrigible.
Ed: Also cynical. Your anniversary card said you love me. I want some proof.

They both laugh and go into a warm embrace which leads to another kiss. Ed closes his eyes, Shirley doesn't. Then Ed opens his eyes and finds himself staring into hers.

Ed: (Breaking from the kiss) That's cheating. You've got your eyes open.
Shirley: I've known you for four years, Edward Swales, and this is the first time I've noticed you've got a gold filling in that back tooth.
Ed: A fellow's entitled to some secrets.
Shirley: Well, it's out in the open now. If we ever get divorced I'll include it in the settlement. I'll want custody of the tooth.
Ed: All right. As long as I get visiting rights at mealtimes.

They both laugh warmly and gaze at each other with obvious love.

Ed: We'll never get divorced. Not you and I, Shirley. We were made for each other. We're the perfect match.
Shirley: You make us sound like a couple of bookends.

Ed: No, there's one big difference between us and bookends. There's nothing to keep us apart.

He grabs her for another embrace. They are deep into a kiss when the phone interrupts them.

Ed: That'll be your sister . . . the perennial bridesmaid — never the blushing bride.
Shirley: Let's hope Bobby takes a shine to her.
Ed: (As he crosses to the phone) Yes, with a bit of luck her blushes could start from tonight.

A similar loving relationship between the other two characters in the show, the very tall Pauline and the very short Bobby, could be built this way. The script will have dealt with how they've been deliberately sat at the dinner table at different times so they wouldn't be on their feet at the same moment and notice the disparity in their heights.

Interior.   The Lounge.   Evening.

The four of them are seated round the dining table finishing their meal.

Ed: I think it's time I proposed a toast. Raise your glasses please. *(They all do so)* To my three year old bride . . . *(Corrects himself)* No, that sounds like I'm child-snatching. I'll rephrase it. To my bride of three years . . . the woman with the warmest heart — and the coldest feet — to Shirley!
All: To Shirley!

They sip their drinks.

Pauline: Another toast. To the happy couple. This is your third anniversary, may you have fifty more.
Bobby: (To Pauline) I'll see your fifty and raise you ten. *(Toasting)* To sixty more.

Shirley and Ed clink their glasses together and Bobby and Pauline do likewise. But Bobby's glass is too high and it tips Pauline's glass over her new dress.

Pauline stands up immediately, upset.

Pauline: My new dress!

Bobby stands up and offers his handkerchief.

Bobby: (Apologising) I'm sorry, it was an accident. Here, use this.

Pauline starts to dab her dress with the handkerchief and it suddenly dawns on both her and Bobby that they are so different in height.

They both turn to Ed and Shirley for an explanation. Ed and Shirley turn to look at each other, embarrassed and unable to think of the right words to say.

Shirley: (To Pauline) I'll wet a teacloth. It'll work better.

She gets up and goes off to the kitchen.

Pauline and Bobby look to Ed.

Ed: I'll help her wet it.

He quickly avoids the situation and follows Shirley into the kitchen.

We stay with Bobby and Pauline who turn back to face each other. She looking down at him and him looking up at her.

There's a short continued embarrassed silence and then Bobby starts to giggle. It builds into a long laugh with Pauline joining in as though it were infectious.

Pauline: Why are we laughing?
Bobby: It's my psychiatrist's idea. He said in an embarrassing situation you should always laugh.

153

It helps break the ice. Mind you, this one could be a whole glacier.

Pauline: (Still laughing) We look like a computer date with the cards all mixed up.

Bobby: Do you want to take your high-heeled shoes off?

Pauline: What for?

Bobby: So I could put them on.

The laughter is gradually dying out.

Bobby: I'm really sorry about your dress.

Pauline: It's all right. I'm sure it'll wash out in time. *(Pause)* I'm sorry too.

Bobby: For what?

Pauline: Being so tall.

Bobby: I don't know why we're apologising to each other. We're the way God made us, right?

Pauline: (More confident) Right.

Bobby: (Looks up to heaven) Even he can make little mistakes.

Pauline: (Referring to herself) And big ones. *(A pause)* Bobby, do you get as embarrassed about your height as I do?

Bobby: Oh sure. But it's never more than suicidal. Occasionally I get a bit uptight, like when I travel by plane and the airline charges me for underweight. Or if I go to the races and they tell me the jockey's entrance is round the back. Still, it has it's compensations. At least I get in for free.

Pauline: It's worse for a girl when fellows have to look up at you. You wind up being a pain in the neck.

Bobby: All right, Pauline, so you're a little too big and I'm a lot too small. So what? We're the people with a definite purpose in life. We're the contrasts. We make the others look more attractive. *(Pauline smiles)* Have you ever seen a psychiatrist about having a complex?

Pauline: No, never.

Bobby: I've got an idea. Let's play doctors. *(Points to couch)* Over there on the couch. *(She doesn't move)* Trust me, I know all about psychiatry. I've been on more couches than Casanova.

As he leads her over to the couch . . .

Cut to:

Interior.   The Kitchen.   Evening.

Ed is peering through the keyhole out into the lounge.

Ed: You're never going to believe this. He's just laid your sister out on the couch. He's talking to her like a psychiatrist.
Shirley: Let me see. *(She moves Ed out of the way and looks through keyhole)* Well, what do you know — Pauline's got a shrink that's shrunk.

Cut back to:

Interior.   Lounge.   Evening.

Bobby is sitting beside the couch with Pauline lying down on it.

Bobby: You're getting the idea now. Big is beautiful. Tell me, who is your favourite author?
Pauline: My favourite author? F. Scott Fitzgerald.
Bobby: You've got good taste. Did you know he was only five foot tall?
Pauline: (Surprised) No, really?
Bobby: I don't know. He may have been six foot two, but would it have made any difference? You still like his work. It's a funny thing, but *Who's Who* never mentions heights, only achievements.
Pauline: You're right. I never thought of that before. You know something, Bobby? *(With affection)* You're a great guy . . . for a little fellow.
Bobby: (Also with affection) That's big of you to say so.

They hold hands.

155

If you imagine Woody Allen playing the part of Bobby you can see where the laughs would be.

*   *   *

This final chapter is aimed at teaching you to sell what you write. And for that you'll need to know where the markets are.

The major script market in Britain is the British Broadcasting Corporation which fills two TV channels on its own. Material for them should be submitted to The Script Department, Light Entertainment, B.B.C. Television, The Television Centre, Wood Lane, London W.12 (01-743 8000).

Scripts intended for the commercial TV Companies should also be addressed to the Light Entertainment Department at the following places:

Anglia Television Ltd, Anglia House, Norwich NR1 3JG. (0603 615151).

Border Television Ltd, The Television Centre, Carlisle, CA1 3NT. (0228 25101)

Central Independent Television PLC, Central House, Broad Street, Birmingham B1 2JP. (021 643 9898)

Channel Four Television Co. Ltd, 56-62, Charlotte Street, London, W.1. (01-631 4444)

Channel Television, Television Centre, Rouge Bouilon, St. Helier, Jersey, Channel Islands. (0534 73999)

Grampian Television Ltd, Queen's Cross, Aberdeen AB9 2XL. (0224 53553)

Granada Television Ltd, Granada TV Centre, Manchester M60 9EA. (061 832 7211)

H.T.V. Ltd, The Television Centre, Bath Road, Brislington, Bristol BS4 3HG. (0272 778366)

London Weekend Television Ltd, South Bank Television Centre, Kent House, Upper Ground, London SE1 9LT. (01 261 3434)

Scottish Television Ltd, Cowcaddens, Glasgow G2 3PR. (041 332 9999)

Television South West Ltd, Derrys Cross, Plymouth PL1 2SP. (0752 663322)

Television South PLC, Television Centre, Northam, Southampton SO9 4YQ. (0703 34211)

Thames Television Ltd, Teddington Studios, Teddington Lock, Teddington, Middlesex TW11 9NT. (01 977 3252)

Tyne Tees Television Ltd, The Television Centre, City Road, Newcastle-Upon-Tyne NE1 2AL (0632 610181)

Ulster Television Ltd, Havelock House, Ormeau Road, Belfast BT7 1EB. (0232 28122)
Yorkshire Television Ltd, The Television Centre, Leeds LS3 1JS. (0532 38283)

Of all the regional commercial TV Channels mentioned you will find that Central TV, Granada TV, London Weekend TV, Thames TV and Yorkshire TV are the largest and therefore have the biggest budgets to buy scripts. Channel Four is not a production company itself. But if it likes your ideas sufficiently it will commission one of the other TV companies to make it for them.

The fees offered for scripts by these companies vary. Yorkshire Television are currently paying new writers £50 per screen minute while the BBC would probably pay about half that amount. As you get more experienced and better known you can command much higher fees.

It is helpful for you to know that when a letter comes from a TV company offering you a certain fee for a quickie, sketch or situation comedy, it *is* just an offer and is quite often negotiable. I know writers who have refused the first offer and got twice as much.

But an initial fee can be but a fraction of the final amount you will end up with on residuals. For instance, you would get half fee again for every repeat in Britain. Some shows are sold to upwards of forty foreign countries and you would get a percentage of your fee for each one. 10% for most countries in Europe other than Germany, 25% for Australia, 75% for Canada, 100% for America and a startling 150% for Germany. British comedy is popular in countries all over the world and a fee of say £20 for a quickie on a Dave Allen show could easily earn you about £150 with the residuals.

Foreign markets are a lucrative source of income for comedy writers. I have sold quickies, sketches and situation comedy scripts direct to TV companies in Austria, Australia, Belgium, Canada, Denmark, Germany, Eire, the Netherlands, Norway, South Africa, Spain, Sweden, Switzerland and America. Shortly I hope to include France and Italy in that list too.

These markets are just as open to you as they were to me. You can write direct to the Head of Light Entertainment sending samples of your work. It can be sent in English, but be sure it does not rely on wordplays or anything too typically British to be understood abroad.

157

Austria. Osterreichischer Rundfunk, ORF-Zentrum Wien, A-1136 Wien, Wurzburggasse 30, Austria.

Australia. Australian Broadcasting Commission, Box 487, G.P.O., Sydney 2001, Australia.

Channel 7 Sydney, Amalgamated Television Services Pty. Ltd., Television Centre, Epping, NSW, Australia 2121.

Belgium. Belgische Radio En Televisie, Omroepcentrum, B-1040 Brussels, Belgium.

Radio Télévision Belge, Cité de la Radio-Télévision, B-1040 Brussels, Belgium.

Canada. Canadian Broadcasting Corporation, P.O. Box 500, Station 'A', Toronto, Ontario M5W 1E6, Canada.

C.T.V. Television Network Ltd., 42, Charles Street East, Toronto, Ontario M4Y 1T4, Canada.

Denmark. Danmarks Radio, TV-Byen, DK-2860 Søborg, Denmark.

Finland. Oy Yleisradio AB, Box 10, SF-00241 Helsinki 24, Finland.

Oy Mainos Reklam AB (MTV), Pasilankatu 44, SF-00240 Helsinki 24, Finland.

France. Télévision Française 1 (TF1), Société Nationale TF1, 15 Rue Cognac Jay, F-75340 Paris, France.

Antenne 2 (A2F), Société Nationale Antenne 2, 5-7 Rue de Montessuy, F-75341 Paris Cedex 07, France.

France Regions 3, (FR3), Société Nationale FR3, 5 Ave. du Recteur-Poincaré, F-75782 Paris Cedex 16, France.

Germany. A.R.D., 8 Munchen 2, Arnulfstrasse 42, Germany.

Zweites Deutsches Fernsehen (ZDF), Essenheimer Landstrasse, D-6500, Mainz-Lerchenberg, Germany.

WDR Fernsehen, Appellhofplatz 1, 5 Köln 1, Germany.

Ireland. Radio Telefis Eireann, Donnybrook, Dublin 4, Eire.

Italy. Radiotelevisione Italiana, Direzione TV, Viale Mazzini 14, 00195 Roma, Italy.

Netherlands. V.A.R.A. Television, Heuvellaan 33, Hilversum, Holland

K.R.O. Television, Postbus 9000, 1201 dh, Hilversum, Holland.

A.V.R.O. Television, Postbus 2, s-Gravelandsweg 52, Hilversum, Holland.

N.C.R.V. Television, Schuttersweg 8-10, Hilversum, Holland.

T.R.O.S. Telelvision, Lage Naarderweg 45-47, 1217 GN, Hilversum, Holland.

New Zealand. Television New Zealand, P.O. Box 3719, Auckland, New Zealand.

Norway. Norsk Rikskringkasting (NRK), Bjørnstjerne Bjørnsons Plass 1, Oslo 3, Norway.
South Africa. English Variety Department, S.A.B.C. TV, P.O. Box 8606, Johannesburg 2000, South Africa.
Spain. Television Española, Apt. de Correos 26002, Madrid 11, Spain.
Sweden. Sveriges Television Ab, TV1, Oxenstiernsgatan 26, Stockholm, Sweden.
Sveriges Television AB, TV2, Oxenstiernsgatan 34, Stockholm, Sweden.
Switzerland. Schweizer Fernsehen, 8052 Zurich, Switzerland.
U.S.A. A.B.C. Television, 1330 Avenue Of The Americas, New York, N.Y. 10019, U.S.A.
C.B.S. Inc., 51 West 52nd Street, New York, N.Y. 10019, U.S.A.
N.B.C., 30 Rockefeller Plaza, New York, N.Y. 10020, U.S.A.

Be sure to keep copies of everything you send. If you get no reply from a foreign TV company write to them after six weeks enquiring about its progress. With British TV companies enquire after three weeks.

You will be wondering whether you need to have an agent to sell your work for you. The answer is that you don't. Agents are very good for negotiating contracts on your behalf. They know the legal jargon and will spot tricky clauses you may not have noticed. If a buyer is late in paying they will put gentle pressure on him to be more prompt. In short, they will protect you and your work and see that you are not exploited or taken advantage of.

For this worthy service they will usually take ten per cent commission on your domestic earnings and up to twenty per cent on foreign sales.

In many cases they do find you work. But some of the big ones I have spoken to do not consider it to be part of their job. They won't hustle for you. Those particular agents will only accept clients who are already well established and able to find their own work.

But there are other agents who are always looking out for new writers with promise. People whose careers they can build.

Here is a list of literary agents who represent some of our top scriptwriters and may agree to take you on their books too:

Roger Hancock Ltd, 8 Waterloo Place, London S.W.1. (01-839-6571)

Fraser & Dunlop Ltd, 91 Regent Street, London W1R 8RU. (01-734-7311)

April Young Ltd, 16 Neal's Yard, Monmouth Street, London WC2H 9DP. (01-240-0111)

Andrew Mann Ltd, 1 Old Compton Street, London, W.1. (01-734-4751)

Norman Payne Agency, 28 Queens Road, Weybridge, Surrey. (97-43657)

Fact and Fiction Agency, 16 Greenway Close, London N.W.9. (205-5716)

William Morris (U.K.) Ltd, 147 Wardour Street, London W.1. (01-743-9361)

Richard Stone, 18 York Buildings, Adelphi, London W.C.2. (01-839-6421)

Harvey Unna Ltd, 14 Beaumont Mews, London W.1. (01-935-8589)

Aza Artists, 652 Finchley Road, London NW11 7NT. (01-458-7288)

If you don't manage to get an agent to take you on right away, don't be disheartened. You can make it on your own.

In *The Television Writer's Handbook* by Constance Nash and Virginia Oakey, there's a quote from Louis Rudolph, a top executive of America's A.B.C. Television, who urges new writers to keep bombarding the Script Department of his company with scripts to consider.

He says, 'If we read a script that shows talent, we may not buy that particular script because the concept may not be right . . . but the minute one shows talent, we're going to jump on that writer. We're going to drag him in here. There is a crying need for writing talent in television and you have no way to convince producers you have talent except through your scripts. Though your script sent speculatively might not be bought, your potential as a writer will be.'

So go to it. Get those comedy thoughts down on paper. Send them in to the addresses I've given you and let the world know there's a top new writer on their way up the ladder of success.

Good luck.

Bibliography

Let me end up with a list of books that I have in my own collection which I think you might find useful. Some were bought in America but can still be ordered in Britain through either your own bookseller or the Buying Section of Foyles Bookshop in Charing Cross Road, London WC2 (Tel: 01-437-5660).

1. **Contacts.** This is a paperback magazine published annually by The Spotlight, 42/43 Cranbourn Street, London WC2H 7AP (Tel: 01-437-7631). It lists every British literary agent with their names and addresses and also every radio and TV Company with a list of their departments and personnel. Costs about £1 and is an essential to every new writer.
2. **Writer's Market.** A big book that lists literally thousands of American outlets for your writing work. Gives details of requirements and payments. It's updated every year. Published by Writer's Digest, 9933 Alliance Road, Cincinnati, Ohio 45242, U.S.A.
3. **Writing for the BBC.** A pocket sized thin paperback published by BBC Publications, 35 Marylebone High Street, London W1M 4AA.
4. **A Practical Manual of Screen Playwriting for Theater and Television Films** written by Lewis Herman and published by New American Library but available through The New English Library Ltd., Barnard's Inn, Holborn, London, E.C.1.
5. **Feature Writing for Newspapers** by Daniel R. Williamson and published by Hastings House Publishers Inc., 10 East 40th Street, New York, N.Y. 10016, USA.
6. **TV Game Shows** by Maxene Fabe and published by Doubleday & Company, Inc., 277 Park Avenue, New York, N.Y. 10017, U.S.A.
7. **The Television Writer's Handbook** by Constance Nash & Virginia Oakey and published by Barnes & Noble Books and can be bought through their parent company Harper & Row, Publishers, Inc., 10 East 53rd Street, New York, N.Y. 10022, U.S.A.
8. **Writing for Television and Radio** by Robert L. Hilliard and published by Hastings House. (Address as per No. 5 above).
9. **The Writer's Job** written by Robert C. Cosbey and published by Scott, Foresman & Company, 1900 East Lake Avenue, Glenview, Illinois 60025, U.S.A.
10. **The Television Writer** written by Erik Barnouw and published by Hill & Wang, New York. (No address given in the book).
11. **Artistes and Their Agents.** This is a thin paperback published regularly (I think once a year) by John Offord Publications, P.O. Box 64, Eastbourne, East Sussex BN21 3LW. (Lists who the agents are of just about every performer in Britain).

12. **TV Guide Almanac.** A very thick paperback with names, addresses and other very useful information about American TV. Published by Ballantine Books, Inc., 201 E.50th St., New York, N.Y. 10022, U.S.A.

13. **Breaking It Up.** A paperback containing the best routines of thirty-one American comedians. It's compiled and edited by Ross Firestone and published by Bantam Books, Inc., 666 Fifth Avenue, New York, N.Y. 10019, U.S.A.

14. **The Story of 'I Love Lucy'** by Bart Andrews. It's a thick paperback with detailed outlines of the plot of every *I Love Lucy* show from 1951 right through to 1960. It's published by Popular Library, Inc., 355 Lexington Avenue, New York, N.Y. 10017, U.S.A.

15. **The TV Game Shows — How to Get On and Win.** Written by Norman Blumenthal and published in paperback by Pyramid Books, Pyramid Communications, Inc., 919 Third Avenue, New York, N.Y. 10022, U.S.A.

16. **How Speakers Make People Laugh.** By Bob Bassindale. A good book to study if you consider writing speeches. It's published by Parker Publishing Company, Inc., West Nyack, N.Y. 10994, U.S.A.

17. **How to Speak and Write With Humor** by Percy H. Whiting. Published by McGraw-Hill Book Company Inc., 1221 Avenue of the Americas, New York, N.Y. 10020, U.S.A.

18. **Writing and Selling Fillers and Short Humor.** Edited by A. S. Burack. Published by The Writer Inc., 8 Arlington Street, Boston, Ma. 02116, U.S.A.

19. **The Best Jokes of All Time and How to Tell Them** by George C. Lewis and Mark Wachs. Published by Hawthorn Books Inc., 260 Madison Avenue, New York, N.Y. 10011, U.S.A.

20. **The Last Laugh** by Phil Berger. This deals with the new wave of club comics who are trying to be different. Published by William Morrow & Company Inc., 105 Madison Avenue, New York, N.Y. 10016, U.S.A.

Appendix of Terms

For your future reference, here are a few of the terms used in scripts which relate to camera shots:

Fade In Where your picture gradually slides into a scene from black.

Fade Out Where your picture gradually slides out of a scene into black.

Cut To . . Where your picture changes to something else instantly.

Mix To *or* **Dissolve** Where the next picture comes in just as the first one is disappearing. It's slower than *Cut To* but quicker than *Fade Out* or *Fade In*.

Close Up A head and shoulders shot.

Medium Shot Usually a shot of a person from the waist up.

Single Shot A shot of one person.

Two-Shot A shot of two people.

Group Shot A shot of a group of people.

Wide Shot *or* **Cover Shot** A shot that will cover the whole scene of action. Can also be called *Establishing Shot*.

Pan When, instead of taking a *Wide Shot* to establish everything at once, you move the camera slowly sideways to reveal things gradually. Say in a police identity parade you could *pan* along the line to show one man at a time.

Dolly In When you move the camera slowly in from, say, a *Medium Shot* to a *Close Up*. This is done a lot when covering a singer.

Dolly Out Moving the camera out from a *Close Up*.

Zoom In Camera simultaneously dollies in and lowers from a high to a low angle.

Zoom Out Camera simultaneously raises and pulls back.

Cross With Him Camera follows actor, panning or tilting as necessary. It means that the shot is ad libbed according to the speed and movement of the actor and whether he crosses behind obstacles that would mean the camera lost sight of him.